Gift Made Possible by
**Medford Friends
of the Library**

JACKSON COUNTY
Library Services

TO COMMIT

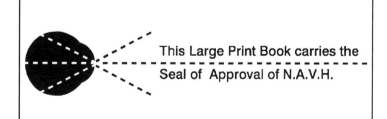

This Large Print Book carries the
Seal of Approval of N.A.V.H.

A BROKEN ROADS ROMANCE

To Commit

Carolyn Brown

THORNDIKE PRESS
A part of Gale, Cengage Learning

GALE
CENGAGE Learning

Detroit • New York • San Francisco • New Haven, Conn • Waterville, Maine • London

GALE
CENGAGE Learning

Copyright © 2008 by Carolyn Brown.
A Broken Roads Romance Series #2.
Thorndike Press, a part of Gale, Cengage Learning.

LIBRARY OF CONGRESS CATALOGING-IN-PUBLICATION DATA

Brown, Carolyn, 1948–
    To commit / by Carolyn Brown.
      p. cm. — (Thorndike Press large print clean reads) (A broken roads romance series ; no. 2)
    ISBN-13: 978-1-4104-1653-7 (alk. paper)
    ISBN-10: 1-4104-1653-4 (alk. paper)
    1. Hotelkeepers—Fiction. 2. Bed and breakfast accommodations—Fiction. 3. Sulphur (Okla.)—Fiction. 4. Large type books. I. Title.
PS3552.R685275T58 2009
813'.54—dc22
                                 2009013880

Published in 2009 by arrangement with Thomas Bouregy & Co., Inc.

Printed in the United States of America
1 2 3 4 5 6 7 13 12 11 10 09

To Dennis, Patti, and Dustyn Russell
with love

CHAPTER ONE

Rusty hinges squeaked like the chirp of a strange exotic bird as the cold north wind swung the homemade sign hanging from the eaves of the roof. From the end of the lane the engraving in the old weathered piece of wood was barely visible. *Brannon Inn, est. 1966.* That was the year Stella's grandmother, Molly Brannon, turned her home into a specialized boarding house and showed her ex-husband she was no longer putting up with his philandering ways. Generation one of a long line of men who couldn't be trusted. Generation two was Stella's own father. *Three?* Well, Stella kept the tradition alive when she also married a scoundrel.

Stella gathered her denim jacket tightly around her and waved at the little boy in the back of the van until she couldn't see his snaggle-toothed grin any more. He'd been the highlight of the party of ten, capturing her heart from the moment he brought his red hair, freckles and feisty attitude through the front door. Stella desperately wanted to kidnap him and run away to a far off island where she could keep him forever. But Thanksgiving was over and it was time to wave good-bye to Jasper. She leaned on the porch post, the brisk fall air fluffing her long blond curls and blowing them around her face. She'd been watching people come and go from Brannon Inn for several months now, but this was the first time she'd had a yearning to change things.

She hung her coat in the hall closet and warmed her hands by the open fire roaring in the big stone fireplace her ancestors built when they constructed the original part of the house. In the beginning it was just one huge room with a sleeping loft upstairs for a couple of newlyweds. Then an ancestor built on a bedroom wing for the children, and another one modernized with indoor plumbing. Now it had two wings — five bedrooms and three bathrooms in one; three bedrooms and two bathrooms in the other. Stella reopened the Brannon Inn the winter before, six weeks after her grandmother died and one month after her husband of five years, Mitch Mason, came in one day and told her she was a hindrance to his acting career.

She pulled her hair back with a rubber band and roped down the naturally blond curls into a ponytail at the nape of her neck. Work waited. Good, hard work that kept her sane. She stripped beds in the five bedrooms in the north wing of the house and shoved a load of sheets into one of three washing machines. Wading across a mountain of dirty towels and linens she picked up a dust cloth on her way back down the hallway. It was just routine cleaning. Dust, then scrub the bathrooms, wipe down the vanities, put freshly ironed doilies on the dressers and homemade mints in the candy dishes on the night stands.

She slipped a country music CD into the portable player and jacked the volume up as high as it would go. *Ultimate Country Party,* a medley of fast-moving tunes that her sister gave her for her birthday a couple of years ago blared. Stella worked up a sweat keeping pace with the music as she cleaned. Shania Twain sang, *Whose Bed Have Your Boots Been Under?* Stella grabbed the dust mop and twirled it around like a partner on the dance floor. She made a clean sweep of the hardwood floor around the queen sized bed and wondered if Mitch was still parking his boots under his agent's bed. The one who'd convinced him that Stella was a hindrance to his career and who'd insisted on a clause in the divorce papers giving Stella back her maiden name. After all Mitch wouldn't want any association with Stella when he made the big time. Giggling aloud, she and the mop did a rendition of a fast two-step. It had been forever since she'd actually been on the dance floor with a good looking man. She dipped and swayed, batted her eyelashes and smiled brightly at the mop.

She was singing louder than Shania when she sashayed backward and bumped right into a man standing in the doorway of the bedroom. The mop clattered to the floor and it took every ounce of willpower she could conjure up to keep from bolting like a jack rabbit flushed out of a thicket by a whole passel of half starved coyotes. She bit the end of her tongue to stifle a scream. Her heart stopped in the middle of a beat and her chest ached as it tried to resume its normal speed.

For just a second when she turned around she thought she was facing Mitch decked out in hunting garb. She wanted to beat him with the mop handle until he was cold and blue. Then she blinked and realized it wasn't Mitch after all. This man, killer or saint, was shorter and actually better looking. Same dark hair and eyes, but with a stronger chin and fuller mouth and thicker across the shoulders with a slimmer waist. Muscular arms held a rifle and deep brown eyes held no humor.

"Who . . . in . . . the . . . devil . . . are . . . you?" she demanded, wondering if he was a terrorist and if he would throw that big gun on his shoulder and aim it right at her fluttering heart. Well, other than Brannon Inn probably supplying him with a fantastic post for his terrorist acts, he'd be disappointed if he did shoot her. There was no money, jewels or other valuables in the house; only a freezer and pantry, both full of food, and a mountain of dirty laundry in the utility room. All of which she'd gladly give him if he wouldn't murder her.

"Who are you? Did Granny Brannon finally take my advice and hire a maid?"

"I am Stella." She pushed a button on the CD player and a deadly silence filled the room where the music had been playing loudly. She stepped right up into his face, her pale blue eyes locking with his dark ones, and neither one blinking. "And what are you doing here? Do you often walk right into a house without even knocking?"

He crossed his arms over his chest and

grinned.

She didn't think any part of him was amusing. Not his black hair. Not those twinkling brown eyes. Not even that that cocky grin on his face.

"A steam train could have crashed through the front door and you wouldn't have heard it. I have reservations for a party of fourteen. Surely you remember talking to me. I'm the one with fourteen hunters for the weekend, and then a single room for two weeks just for me. And where is Granny?"

"She passed away last year, and I most certainly did not talk to you."

His cocky grin faded. "Well, honey, I talked to someone, and I've got thirteen more hunters out there in your front room waiting to be shown a room to stow their gear." An aura of pure ice exuded from his words and Stella battled the urge to hug herself to keep the chill away. Were all dark haired men just natural rascals?

Stella bowed up to him again, her nose just inches from his. "Brannon Inn belongs to me and I'm the one who makes reservations. I don't have a secretary or a receptionist. And you do *not* have reservations here for this weekend much less for two whole weeks."

"Check your books — lady." He drawled

the last word out so long it sounded like something tainted and dirty. "I talked to a woman who said she was writing it down. Fourteen of us for the weekend. Breakfast on the sideboard and supper around the big table. I gave her my credit card number and while you are checking you'll find I'm your boarder for two whole weeks."

And your neighbor for a hell of a lot longer than that, he thought but kept that to himself. Thank goodness the house on his new property was a quarter of a mile away from this shrewish woman.

She pushed her way past him and headed to the desk in the great room. She opened the registration book and pushed it in front of him. "You're dreaming. See? Blank until next weekend."

He flipped a page back and there were several names penciled in. Then he turned a page ahead and there was his name, party number and what they wanted. He turned it back around, practically shoving it under her nose. "Rance Harper and his band of merry hunters at your service ma'am. Someone must have turned two pages at once."

Lauren, she thought as she stared at the name and numbers in her sixteen year old niece's handwriting. Lauren had spent a few

13

days at the inn during the holidays and must have taken the call. *Where was I?* Then she remembered going to the grocery store that morning while her sister, Maggie, and Lauren packed to leave.

He raised a dark eyebrow at her. "So?"

She looked at the gang of men standing behind him. "So, it's an honest mistake, okay? Go play Rambo in the woods and by supper time I'll have your rooms ready and supper on the table. Leave your gear right there until you get back."

"Yes, ma'am," Rance saluted sharply, making fun of her and chalking up a feather for his war bonnet. "We'll be back at five thirty. Is supper still at six?"

"Yes, it is." She nodded, angry at the whole world for tossing this piece of work in her lap. She'd looked forward to a few days to regroup and recoup from a busy six weeks. And there stood more than a dozen men. It would be like cooking for Goliath and his army of giants. Well, they would have good wholesome food in front of them and they'd have clean beds and toilet paper in the bathrooms, but not one word in the travel brochures said she had to like it or even smile brightly at them when she set their iced tea beside their plates at the supper table.

Rance tipped his hat at her. "Okay guys. Drop your bags and we'll be off to the woods. We'll see you at supper time, ma'am. And I'm real sorry about Granny Brannon. She was a wonderful old girl. I might have asked her to marry me just for her cooking if she'd been a little younger."

"Granny had the good sense to never trust a scoundrel." Stella smarted off but it brought her little satisfaction. The humor in his deep laughter still haunted her an hour later as she finished remaking all the beds in the north wing and opened the doors in the south wing to inspect the rooms which hadn't been used in two weeks. Eight bedrooms and Lauren's note said they wanted all of them.

"Blast it all to Hades on a silver poker!" She swore under her breath and pulled a big aluminum stock pot from under the cabinet. She'd make a pot of chili for supper. At least the insolent dark haired rogue hadn't told Lauren exactly what the menu should be, so if there were a few weak stomachs amongst the great white hunters, then they'd just have to go to bed hungry or spend the night wolfing down antacids.

She whipped up a German chocolate cake and two pecan pies for dessert, and checked the freezer to be sure there was enough ice cream to dress up either one. Then she put a rising of bread on the cabinet to make cinnamon buns for breakfast.

Stella had fallen into the work at Bannon Inn naturally. It didn't seem to matter if she cooked for one man or for fifteen men, or a group of eight complete with whining kids. It was all just readjusting recipes and the realization that these people paid a lot better than her ex-husband. Besides, not one of them was ever going to walk in the kitchen and tell her she was an obstruction to his almighty wannabe career like her ex-husband had done.

The aroma of chili powder and fresh pecan pies combined in the kitchen and she felt a tiny surge of guilt for the way she'd snapped at Mr. Rance whoever. If his hair wasn't as black as Mitch's and his eyes even darker, and if he hadn't scared the bejesus right out of her, she might not have bowed up to him so staunchly. She gave herself a stinging lecture, in a thinking tone of severity with her grandmother's voice, that customers were what paid her bills.

She opened the cabinet doors and took another stock pot from the assortment of shiny pots and pans, filled it half full of water, added two whole chickens and a half dozen bouillon cubes. She'd give them a

16

choice. Chicken and dumplings or chili, or both if they were really hungry after chasing a whole herd of deer all over the southern part of the state. If they wanted they could even mix the two together. She shuddered at the idea, but a smile raised her spirits from the depths of pure unadulterated wrath to a more pleasant level.

The sun was setting in the West, filtering through the lace curtains and casting a warm glow on the dining room table when the guests arrived. She heard their trucks, then conversation as they stomped up on the wooden porch. In the spring when the fishermen arrived, they'd eat supper and then sit on the wide verandah, spinning tales about catfish or bass or striper as big as an Angus steer that broke a million pound tests line and swam back through the creeks and rivers to the ocean. But in the fall and winter the deer, turkey or squirrel hunters ate their supper with the gusto of hungry hounds and sat in front of the fireplace, telling stories of bucks the size of Big Foot who ran off into the woods with bullets piercing every major organ. They'd declare that they followed a blood trail for sixteen miles and never caught sight of the eighty-nine point rack again. They'd swear on their grandma's eyes that super-buck jumped a barbed wire fence into restricted property or he'd be mounted and hung on their den wall.

She'd heard every story there was to tell. Maybe that's why Jasper, in all his wide eyed innocence, had made such an impression on her. The squirrels playing in the trees behind the Inn had mesmerized him and he didn't even throw up a finger, point at them and yell, "Bang!"

A tall red haired fellow with clear blue eyes took his dirty boots off just inside the door. "Mmmm, this house smells wonderful. Is that really chili?"

Rance sniffed the air. "No, you dummy, it's boiling chicken. It probably won't be as good as Granny Brannon's but it sure smells good."

Another hunter raised his chin and sniffed the air. "Chili. I'm an expert on good chili. A connoisseur if you please and there's no way that smell is chicken, Rance."

A short, plump fellow with a bald spot on the back of his head, piped up. "It's cake. Chocolate, right?"

She struck a match and lit a dozen votive candles strewn down the middle of the table. "It's all of the above. Served in exactly thirty minutes. If you're not here at six o'clock then you may get left out. So pick up your gear and decide which rooms you want. Five on this end. Three on the other."

Rance reached for a soft leather suitcase and matching boot bag. "I'll take the last one on this wing. Carl can have the last room on that wing, and the rest of you can fight over who gets to sleep the farthest away from his snoring. But fighting takes time, so you better hurry up or you'll be left out in the cold, starving to death."

Twenty minutes later she ladled chili into three serving bowls and spaced them down the length of the long wood table. She did the same with crock bowls of steaming chicken and dumplings. Granny Brannon always said chicken and dumplings were to be served in crock bowls; never clear glass. Stella wished she'd asked her why as she filled the empty areas on the table with platters of piping hot corn bread and yeast rolls, along with a tray of cheese and pickles and one of carrot and celery sticks.

A group of dirty men dressed in camouflage disappeared to the north and south ends of the house and in half an hour, a bunch of clean shaven, nice smelling men emerged in their places. The change always amazed her. The way to a man's heart was truly through his stomach.

"Mighty fine looking vittles, Miss Stella," the tall red haired fellow said.

"Thank you. You'd all best start passing those bowls before everything gets cold. Two things in the world that aren't worth eating are chili with a skim of grease on the top, or chicken and dumplings when the steam is gone. I've got water, sweet tea, unsweet tea, and hot coffee." She pulled a small wooden cart laden with glass pitchers and an insulated carafe of coffee around the table.

One of the men filled his bowl with chili and sighed in appreciation with the first bite. "Best chili I've ever tasted and I know my chili. And the cornbread is good enough to be cake."

Another loaded his plate with dumplings. "But not chocolate cake. I smelled chocolate. I swear I did."

"Got to clean up your plate, though, or there'll be no dessert. Granny Brannon told me that for years. From the first time I came to Murray County to deer hunt with my dad," Rance said.

The red haired man blew on another spoonful of chili. "Bet you could make venison chili. I sure wish my wife would fix venison for me. Lord, but I love a good deer roast, but she won't have it in the house."

"Well, what did you expect when you married that city girl, Bill? Hey, Miss Stella, you ever made a venison roast? By the way, my

20

name is Carl."

"Yes, I have. Need a refill on that tea? Was it sweet or not?" She asked Rance.

"Sweet." Rance held up his glass and watched her pour. She could have been an English princess serving tea in a castle with all that gorgeous blond hair and those haunting big, blue eyes beneath heavy dark lashes that didn't go with her hair. But Rance wasn't about to fall for a tall blond again. Not ever. Even if he ever did find a dark haired little angel, he would check himself into a psyche ward before he thought about the commitment word. Maybe when he was eighty or ninety and had forgotten the pain of the first marriage he'd let someone talk him into the "C" word. He'd learned his lesson and though he'd been called lots of names in his lifetime, nobody had ever said Rance was stupid.

He reached up to take the glass of tea from her and their fingertips brushed ever so slightly. The sparks dancing around could have rivaled the Fourth of July fireworks show at the Sulphur High School football stadium. Stella had never experienced anything like it from a mere touch. It terrified her: she thought she'd buried anything remotely like desire several months before in Hollywood, California.

Carl rubbed his chin in deep thought. "Miss Stella, you reckon if we brought a couple of haunches of deer in here before we take the meat down to the locker you might fix it for us for supper tomorrow night?"

"I suppose so. What do you do with it if you don't take it home to eat?" She asked.

"Oh, we give it to that charity to feed the hungry folks," Bill said. "We take it to a locker plant and they process it and give it to the needy."

"That's pretty decent of you. Yes, I'll make you venison. How many did you get today?"

"I got a big buck. Nice rack. I'm having it mounted for the den."

That was as much or more than Stella wanted to know. Other than a few children, Jasper included, she seldom encouraged her guests to tell her their personal stories. But somehow before they left she knew too much every time.

"Well, bring a couple of big roasts in here after supper. I guess you've got the deer hog dressed and ready to go to the locker in the morning?"

"Yep, hanging out in the smoke house." Rance nodded. "Granny always said that's where to put it. Have things changed?"

"No, nothing has changed. That's the place to put the kill or scale the fish in the spring. You're responsible to keep it clean, just like when she was running the business." Stella removed dishes as they finished and shed them to the kitchen on her cart.

Rance helped carry the last of the plates that wouldn't fit on the cart. "What happened to Granny Brannon? I've been coming here to hunt since I was sixteen. My dad brought me the first time. Last year we lost Dad just before hunting season and I just couldn't make myself go without him."

"Granny had cancer," Stella said.

"You buy the place?"

"No, she left it to me, not that it's any of your business," Stella said. "Since you're in here, take that stack of clean plates to the table and I'll bring out the pecan pies and German chocolate cake."

The fellow at the end of the table rubbed his chubby little hands together. "I told you. I knew it. Chocolate. German chocolate with nuts and coconut. I'm going to be miserable and love every minute of it."

Stella shook her head in amazement. Hunters. Fishermen. Families. Their faces changed and their gender, but their appetite for good food never did. She cut a huge wedge of triple layered cake and gently laid it on a plate. "With or without ice cream?"

"With and a piece of pecan pie, too." His eyes sparkled.

One of the hunters opted for pecan pie. "Tommy would love this. That's my ten year old son and he thinks pecan pie is the 'bestest thing in the whole world.' Want to see his picture? When he's twelve, he's coming with us." With the expertise of a proud father he deftly removed his wallet from his pocket and flipped it open to show Stella the picture of a tow headed kid in a baseball uniform.

"Only child?" She asked.

Rance answered for him. "Yep. Tommy is all boy. It takes a dozen people to keep up with him."

Bill shoved his wallet into her hands. "Hey, looky here at my kids. I got a set of twins that could scale a glass door on a rainy day."

"Good looking girls." Stella looked and handed it back. "They can't be that ornery, though. They look like angels."

Rance chuckled and she shot him a dirty look. "Hey, don't look at me like that, lady. He's the one who said they were devils in disguise," he said, pointing to Bill.

"That's right. And my wife is expecting another one. Thank goodness we've got a good nanny." Bill put his wallet away, but the dam had already broken and everyone had out a picture for her to see. So, they were all married men with kids who liked cake or were angels with wives at home who didn't cook venison.

When she'd seen them all she looked up at Rance, fully expecting him to have his pictures out. Would his children have that jet black hair and dark eyes or maybe they'd take after their mother who was — what?

"End of the line of proud daddies," he blushed slightly.

"Cake, pie or both?" She asked instead of pursuing the discussion with him.

Bill hooted and Carl put his hand over his full mouth. "You sure wouldn't want to show off your pictures. Miss Stella wouldn't be a bit interested in those two babies of yours. They're so spoiled it's pitiful."

Rance's neck rapidly turned scarlet. "Hush, Carl. At least my babies don't try to scale a glass wall on a rainy day. Now let's take a flashlight out to the smoke house and carve out a couple of roasts for Stella to put in some kind of magic sauce. You must use your Granny's dumpling recipe because these are just like I remember. I'll have pecan pie."

She deliberately touched his hand when

she served the pie and the jolt almost glued her to the floor again. It hadn't been a freak accident after all. It wasn't fair: he was married. To have those kind of feelings awakened anew, and with a married man. Some days it just didn't pay to get out of bed.

Rance swallowed hard, amazed that his voice sounded almost normal. "Bet you can make a venison roast just like Granny did, too."

After two shocks of nothing more than pure desire shooting through his veins, he figured he'd sound like a prepubescent kid with a high squeaky voice. Stella was one fine looking, well-put-together woman, but he'd vowed long ago never to get tangled up with another tall blond, not even if she was an angel straight from heaven with white wings and an untarnished halo. Rance Harper did not go back on his vows. Not for anything or anyone. Not even for his heart.

"I'll try to make it taste like Granny's," she said. "Snacks will be on the sideboard for the evening in case anyone gets the munchies. Television has cable, and when I get the kitchen cleaned up, I'm off to my quarters and you gentlemen are on your own. Breakfast is on the bar from five o'clock until six."

She sautéed a cup of sliced onions in real butter then slowly browned the venison in the same deep skillet. When both sides were seared she added a cup of beef broth, put a lid on the heavy cast iron kettle and set it inside the refrigerator to marinate overnight. Tomorrow she would cook it in a slow oven and then add potatoes and carrots an hour before she was ready to serve it. A big basket of hot rolls and a salad would complete their supper. Maybe she'd make a deep dish apple pie and serve it warm with cinnamon ice cream.

The men were engrossed in the football game on television and stories of the big bucks during commercials when she climbed the stairs to the loft which was her own private world; a bedroom/sitting room combination with her grandmother's four-poster bed on one wall, a comfortable sofa facing the sliding glass doors onto an upstairs balcony over the garage, and a small bathroom. On the third wall, not covered with furniture or glass doors were floor-to-ceiling bookcases filled with her favorite authors.

She chose an old friend from the bottom shelf, a Sue Grafton, and opened the worn pages to begin reading it again. She finished five pages then gazed out at the winter stars twinkling in the dark sky. She picked the book up again and realized she didn't know what she'd read or where she'd stopped. Her thoughts kept going back to Rance and his dark, brooding eyes. A tickling sensation deep down in her very soul disturbed her. Even if he had awakened the sleeping desires, she had to stop thinking about the man. He, like all the other men in the hunting party, was married and had children.

Finally she laid the book aside and took a long cool shower, set her alarm clock and picked up the phone.

"Dee, were you asleep?" She asked her best friend.

"No, just getting out of the shower. Jack is working on the computer. He's at the stage in his invention where if I breathe too heavy it disturbs him. But, hey, that's the way he brings in all those big beautiful dollars. I'm not complaining. What's going on?"

"I've got a boarder, Matter of fact every room is filled but this one . . ."

"Aha, one has gotten around your cold heart, huh? Who is he and what's his name? Want me to come over right now or wait until morning?" Dee asked.

"He's married and he looks like my ex," Stella said.

"Then take a cold shower and forget

about him."

"I already had one and it didn't work."

"Then take another one and no, you can not have a married man. Especially one that looks like your ex. Sorry, darlin'," Dee said.

"How come I'm not surprised you'd say that? Come around for coffee and pecan pie in the morning. Jack can use the time to finish his project. Good night."

"For pecan pie I'll be there whether he's finished or not. Bye now."

"See you tomorrow," Stella hung up and went back to the shower.

CHAPTER TWO

Dee ate pecan pie and watched Stella cut fresh fruit for a salad. "I want the scoop. I heard he's staying two whole weeks. How'd he ever get under your skin? I thought you were never going to look at another man."

"This coming from the girl who was married six months after her divorce," Stella said.

Dee cut a second piece of pecan pie and refilled her coffee cup. "Annulment. I'm not a divorced woman. I was never married. I lived seven years in sin. Think God and Roxie will forgive me for that?"

Stella nodded. "God might. Roxie's a lot tougher. She and Granny Molly and Etta were the queens of the bed and breakfast establishments in Murray County, you know, and their rules are stricter than God's."

"Oh yes, I know. Not a day goes by Roxie doesn't remind me that she's my grandmother and all southern ladies respect their grandmothers, and that she's one of the three old bed and breakfast queens in the area. You miss Molly don't you? You have to, because I do, and she was your grandmother. Roxie and Etta miss her terribly. Lord, I can't even think of life without Roxie. She drives me crazy sometimes but I love her."

"Yes, I do miss Granny. So much it hurts. Some days it seems like she's right here in the room with me, telling me what to put in a recipe. Other times I want her to be here and realize she's gone. But back to Rance. He's the prettiest thing I've ever seen and he makes my knees turn into Jell-O and my heart do double time and he's married and why do I always have to pick the ones who are either rascals or unavailable," Stella whined. "It's not fair. You got Jack and ya'll have a baby coming. I want those things too, but . . ."

"But you can't have them with a married man, darlin', and what on earth changed your mind? Last week you were going to be an old hermit who ran this boarding house until one Monday morning you dropped dead after having fourteen guests for two solid weeks. At least I think that's the right number," Dee said.

"He did. Rance changed my mind and I didn't have a thing to do with it. I guess it's time to get back into the dating game. But, Dee, I'm twenty six years old and it's awkward."

"Yes, it is. I'm glad Jack was my best friend and he was there when I came home. We kind of just fell into love without all the folderol around it." Dee licked the last remnants of the pie from her fork and eyed the rest of the pie. With a sigh, she decided two pieces were enough. Her obstetrician would have a fit if she gained another five pounds by next week.

Stella sipped her hot tea. "You fell into it. Jack never fell out of it. He's been in love with you since third grade."

"I know. It's mind boggling. Hate to eat and run but that's what I'm going to do. Who else besides this Rance have you got tonight? Want to come down to Roxie's for a lemonade and watch the sunset?"

Stella shook her head. "I'd love to but I've got five bikers. Big old burly men who look like they are part of Hell's Angels but aren't anything but teddy bears in leather. And a bunch of hikers. Mommie dearest. Daddy darling. A girl that looks like she poses for the front of one of those shape up magazines and a couple of sons."

"Been eyeing Rance, has she?"

"Oh, hush and eat and run," Stella frowned.

Dee could get right to the root of things, even when they were kids, and it always came out witty. Cute, short and funny. That was Dee. Stella was the gangly, long legged, horsy one without a graceful bone in her body. Last year, Dee's husband came home one day and announced they were no longer married. He and his rich folks had just had a seven year marriage annulled so he could marry his old high school sweetheart who was pregnant with his child. Dee told Stella that she'd decided to never trust another man. Jack changed that tune real fast. He'd been her best friend forever and lived right next door to the grandmother who'd raised both Dee and her sister, Tally. Roxie's B&B; that stood for Roxie's Bed and Breakfast, or Roxie's Bellyachin' and Blessin's, depending on who was talking. Jack and Dee had fallen in love and been married a little longer than Stella had run the Brannon Inn.

"Call me tonight after Mr. Hunk goes to bed. We'll talk." Dee grabbed a chocolate chip cookie from the jar on the table and waved.

"This is a pretty nice little set up you got

here. Rustic and homey. Bet you get lots of hunters and fishermen," the young woman meandered around the dining room.

"Quite a few." Stella spread a lace tablecloth on the long table and scattered a few candles in brass holders randomly down the middle.

"Mind if I do a few stretching exercises before supper?"

"Not at all," Stella said.

It didn't take a rocket scientist or even a person with an IQ in the single digits to figure out Jewel was waiting on Rance. The rest of the family was still in their rooms, but Jewel had stowed her gear in a hurry and was back in the dining room before Stella could turn around twice. Jewel in a pair of jeans and a sweatshirt was pretty amazing. Tight fitting little hiking britches and a sweater at least two sizes too small would make any man's eyes spin around in his head.

Stella tried not to watch her do leg lifts or hook her toes under the edge of the sofa and do sit ups at a nice slow pace. But she kept stealing glances toward the lady.

I'd be ready to dial 911 on the third sit up. Wait until Rance comes in and sees that piece of work in action. I'll probably have to supply a drooling bowl beside his and those five bikers' plates tonight.

Stella had taken extra pains with her hair, brushing it up into a French twist; she'd even applied a little makeup. She'd splashed on some of the cologne her mother had given her for Christmas the year before. Then she'd gotten angry at herself for the effort. Rance Harper was married and had two children. Lord, why did she have to be attracted to rogues and rascals? Besides if he wasn't married or didn't have children, she'd sure enough take a back seat to the competition in the living room.

"Speak of the devil." She murmured when she heard the crunch of tires in the front yard. He'd said he would be back in time for supper and he was right on time.

She had a bunch of hikers on one wing that ate no meat and preferred fresh vegetables and nothing, absolutely nothing with preservatives. On the other wing she had five big strapping men, four motorcyclists who'd booked in for one night, and Rance. All of whom thought there were three food groups — beefsteak, pork sausage and chili. She mentally drew a line down the middle of the dining room table cloth. Hikers on this end with the wooden bowl of fresh salad and a loaf of warm whole wheat bread, along with a spinach lasagna with low-fat cheese. Bikers and Rance on the other with twice baked potatoes topped with shredded cheddar cheese, crumbled bacon bits, sweet cream butter and pure sour cream, along with a platter of medium rare grilled T-bone steaks and a salad tossed with her special Brannon Inn dressing.

Rance opened the front door. "I'm here. And it smells wonderful."

Stella's heart picked up a thumping beat when he walked in the door. She had to work to keep focused on the table. It was definitely time for her to think about dating, but how could she get back into that whirlwind circle again after more than five years? She was twenty six years old and the last time she went out with anyone was when Mitch swept her off her nineteen year old feet and asked her to marry him. One thing for danged sure, when she got ready to go out again, it wouldn't be with someone who had jet black hair and ebony eyes. She didn't care if he had a personality of gold and a bank roll big enough to buy the state of Texas. She would find a nice, stable blond haired man with light eyes, maybe even one who stuttered or had some other imperfection; someone most definitely with no desires to be an actor.

If nobody else wants him, then why would

you? Granny Brannon's voice was as clear as if she was actually standing right behind her. *I told you that when you were sixteen and you came in here whining and carrying on about that rascal, Joel Curtis. Remember? He was flirting with that hussy who worked at the Sonic and you got jealous.*

"Oh, hush," Stella mumbled.

"Didn't say a word. Steaks look wonderful. Would you like to come live with me and cook for me every day?" Rance joked.

He'd dreamed of Stella the past three nights. He had to keep reminding himself on an hourly basis that he wasn't going to get serious again about any woman; especially a tall blond haired goddess. But dang it all, this woman was getting under his skin.

He'd been standing so close she could feel the warmth of his breath on her bare neck and the smell of his aftershave was intoxicating. She didn't like the shivers playing chase down her back bone. "Mr. Harper, it wouldn't be a good idea for me to be your cook. I'd poison you. Go find a place at the table. I'm loading the tea cart and then it is ready."

"Can't blame a man for trying," he said.

His slow drawl not only made her heart skip a beat but infuriated her so much she would have liked nothing better than to

37

throw the whole platter of steaks at him. She wouldn't even flinch about the waste. That she was attracted to him was bad enough; that he, a married man, was flirting blatantly with her meant he had no scruples or morals. He wasn't a bit better than Mitch.

The Carpenter family paraded in and Jewel joined them at the end of the table away from the repulsive steaks. Stella gritted her teeth at the silly grins on all five men. Every one of them, Rance included, looked like they'd gladly trade their steaks for a chunk of spinach lasagna if they could sit beside the pretty dark haired lady who batted her eyelashes with the expertise of a professional hustler. Hosting two parties at one time wasn't ever easy, but Stella could already tell this was going to be an out and out chore.

And does that make you mad? Not at all! She can be the entertainment tonight. She can fall down on the floor and do crunchies to tighten up those already taut muscles in her tummy, and they can lay bets on how many she can do before she gets bored. Bet she sees to it that Rance wins the pot. She looks like she could eat him for dessert whether he's made of red meat or not!

"And what got you all into hiking?" A

biker asked.

Mrs. Carpenter explained as she filled her plate and passed the food on to her husband. "We started hiking back when Jewel was a Brownie. She needed to hike so many miles to get her patch. We all enjoyed it so much that we've made it a family thing and kept it up. That was nearly seventeen years. She was six that first year and she's twenty three now. By the way Mrs. Brannon, this looks like really good lasagna and it proves a body doesn't have to have all that nasty meat to survive."

"Well, this body does," Rance chuckled. "My body would shrivel up and die without steak."

Jewel gave Rance a sexy sideways glance that said she'd like to use up a lot of energy romping around a big old king sized bed with him. "Why should anything have to die so that I can eat? I'm a vegetarian. I hike to keep this body toned and fit. We're getting ready for a big serious hike up in the Ouachita Mountains in a few months. We're going to do a big portion of the Talimena Trail. It'll take a lot of stamina."

Rance raised an eyebrow. "Oh?"

Stella wanted to spill the whole pitcher of sweet tea in his lap or dump it on Jewel's head. His wife was probably a sweet little stay-at-home mother who had no idea he was a first rate rascal, flirting with two women at a time.

Jewel's eyes sparkled. "Oh, yes, those mountains will give us a workout. I'm also into body building and this weekend is going to be a test to see if it's all been worthwhile. We're going over to the Arbuckle Mountains by Davis. They're not very big, but it'll be good exercise for one day. We usually do a lot of hiking around Grapevine Lake. Got some really good trails there but we thought we'd try this area for a change of pace. Then we're coming back in the early spring to do it again. Probably just before Easter weekend."

"Well good luck," Rance said. "Stella, honey, would you pour me another glass of sweet tea. This steak is perfect. Cooked just like me and my grandpa like them: shoot the bull, wait 'til the bellow dies, carve out a steak and get it hot on the grill."

Honey? Don't you call me honey, you scoundrel. You got a wife at home and two babies. You sit there and flirt with Jewel, and then call me honey, like we're old friends.

"Of course, Mr. Harper." She picked up the unsweetened tea.

"No, sweet tea, honey. I like my tea just like my women — sweet."

Stella shot him a drop-dead look.

Rance downed a fourth of the tea. "Now, Jewel, what were you saying about the mountains over by Davis?"

"They're not so big but it'll be a nice workout. Tell me about you. What are you doing here? Are you married?" She asked.

"Divorced and going to stay that way. Fool me once, shame on you. Fool me twice, makes me a fool," he said.

"Got any kids?" Jewel asked.

Stella cleared the rest of the table and went to the kitchen for desserts. Chocolate cream pie for the hunters. A bowl of fresh fruit topped with a special white chocolate pudding mixed with apricot nectar for the hikers. She strained to hear his answer about children.

"No kids. So what brings you guys to this part of the world?" He turned from Jewel and asked the bikers.

George, the one sitting closest to him, answered. "We're on vacation. Left our families at home for a week and we're riding through Oklahoma, Texas, Louisiana, Florida and then straight back up to Tulsa where we're from. We're just hoping for good weather. Bet we don't stay anywhere in the whole trip where the food is this good, though. Miss Brannon, would you

41

come along with us and cook just for us?"

Stella glanced at Rance. "Sorry, I've got a boarder for two weeks or I might be tempted."

"Is that you she's talking about? Are you staying here for two weeks for real?" George asked.

"I guess I am," Rance nodded.

"Then you'd best lock your door tonight. Old Red there might decide to remove the only obstacle in the path of his good food," George laughed.

Jewel pretended to shiver. "Oh, my, what a thing to say!" she brought the attention back to her with a fake shudder and a big eyed innocent look.

"Now little lady, I was just joshing," he said.

"I know you were, but it sounded so real. Would you be interested in a little moonlight walk?" She looked from the biker to Rance.

"No thanks. I'm worn out. It's been a long day. I'll probably fall asleep before the news is finished tonight," Rance said.

It had been a long, long day and he was ready for sleep, but it didn't come around the second he laid his head on the pillow. Stella's face kept appearing every time he shut his eyes. Finally, he got up, picked up a Sue Grafton mystery novel and read until midnight.

Steam rose off the hot water in the claw-footed tub in Stella's bathroom. She slid down further, letting the deep layer of bubbles cover everything but her face. She could hear Jewel's giggles in the living room as the conversation centered around her and the hike tomorrow.

I don't give a tiny rat's rear if they laugh and talk to that little dark haired, well-built, egotistical girl all night. Her nose is too big and her eyes too close together. She would probably be fat if she didn't run and exercise all the time. A steak would make her round as Santa Claus. Stop it! You are acting like a fourteen year old kid, not an adult.

She could hear the men's tone change from spicy to business in a moment. One minute they were laughing and talking to Jewel, the next, a dull monotone discussing biking, hunting, football and whatever they were watching on the television set drifted up the stairs to her quarters. Evidently, the pretty girl had gone to her room. After all a well-oiled, toned, tanned and mean machine like her young body needed its rest to be able to function on the mountainous hike through the fierce Arbuckle Mountains after breakfast tomorrow morning. Then when her body was at its best she could come back to the Brannon Inn and flirt to her heart's content with divorced Rance Harper who hated tall blondes and lied about having kids.

His buddies had teased him the first night about having two kids that were ornery and tonight he'd said he had no kids. So the man was a three time loser — divorced, a liar, and looked entirely too much like Mitch.

Stella soaked until the water was cold and the bubbles flat but still couldn't get rid of the restlessness upsetting her indifferent world. For the past several months she'd booked clients, cooked meals, poured tea, cleaned up the mess, and started all over again. She pasted a smile on her face and listened to jokes, looked at family pictures and watched hundreds of people come and go, in and out of Brannon Inn. And somehow she found peace in monotony. However, since the day she backed into Rance, she'd been downright edgy and she darned sure didn't like it. Even if her world was a faint shade of gray, with no pure white episodes or midnight black experiences, she liked it that way.

"Divorced," she mumbled. "Once bit,

twice wise. Me, too, Rance. Me, too."

What was Rance Harper's story?

Why do I even care? He might have warmed my cold, hard heart but in ten more days he'll be gone from Brannon Inn and I'll never see him again. After his two week hunting trip, he'll go home to wherever he lives and I'll settle back into my rut. And those ten days can't come too fast!

With that settled she stepped out of the lukewarm water and dried off. She pulled on a pair of black leggings and red socks, topped it with an oversized red plaid, flannel shirt and was buttoning the last button when the phone rang.

"Brannon Inn," she said.

"Stella Brannon?" A masculine voice said. "Is this the Stella Brannon who graduated from Sulphur High School a few years ago?"

"Who is this?"

The voice sighed loudly. "My heart hurts. To think you wouldn't remember my voice. Truly, Stella, I am in pain."

Oh, spare me!

"I'm sorry but I really don't know who I'm talking to," she said.

"Joel. Your old Joel Curtis at your service, ma'am," he said in a soft, sexy drawl. "I just moved back to Sulphur this past week and found out you were running your granny's business."

"My business. Brannon Inn belongs to me now. So where have you been Joel?"

Talk about thinking of the devil and he doth appear.

"Here and there, but you know the old saying about the apple never falling far from the tree and all hearts go home eventually. I'm back in business with my father," he said.

"So where is here and there?"

"Texas, mainly. Brownsville, to be more specific. Hey, are you free for dinner this week. We could have a steak at Two Frogs in Ardmore?"

"No, thanks," she said.

"Hey, surely you're grown up enough not to hold old grudges?" He sounded just as cocky as he had in their junior year of high school.

"Yep, but not foolish enough to repeat the same mistakes."

"Someone said your marriage to the actor didn't work. I'm sorry, Stella, for real, I am. My marriage didn't work either. That's part of the reason I'm back in Sulphur. We could swap stories and . . ."

A long silence followed.

And what? And come back to the Inn for a nice little nightcap. I remember your style,

Joel. You don't just kiss and tell. You kiss and brag.

"You still there?" He asked.

"Yes, and no. Yes, I'm still here Joel, but no, I don't want to go out with you."

"Okay, maybe I'll run by sometime and you can give me a tour of the Inn. I picked you up there for our last date. I don't think your granny ever did really like me," he said.

And I should have listened to her more often.

"That was a long time ago. Nice talking to you, Joel. Tell your momma I said hello." She was easing the receiver down to the cradle when she changed her mind.

"Joel, you still there?" She asked hurriedly.

"Still here. Second thoughts? I promise I'm a little more adult than I was at seventeen," he said.

"I've got guests for supper every night for the next two weeks, but I'd be willing to go for ice cream at eight tomorrow night if that would work with your plans."

"Pick you up at eight then?"

"That would be nice. See you then."

"Thanks, Stella, I'll look forward to seeing you again."

"Me, too." She said, but her heart didn't melt or do flip flops or even skip a single beat. The last time she dated Joel was the year they went to East Central State University in Ada, Oklahoma, along with half the graduating class of Sulphur High School. He was six feet tall, thick blond hair, big blue eyes, an ego bigger than his silver belt buckle and a brazen attitude that drew women to him like bees to honey.

She opened the French doors out onto the balcony, sending a couple of squirrels scampering up the pecan tree overshadowing the back of the Inn. She wrapped one of her granny's quilts around her and snuggled in a chaise lounge.

So Rance was divorced. So was she and so was Joel. The more she tried to sort through the confusion, the more muddled the whole thing became. She had accepted a date with Joel, the man she ended up hating in college. Every time she was in the same room with Rance, her hormones went into overtime. Would Joel affect her that way also?

Stella twirled the back of her hair up into a clip, letting the ends cascade down her neck line. She chose a long column dress of brushed denim with wooden buttons down the side. She left the last four buttons undone for walking ease and picked up her knee high suede boots. Butterflies danced in her stomach like a band of gypsies around a bonfire.

Twenty-six wasn't so old to be dating. Some women didn't even think of marriage until they were well past thirty, and the statistics said there were lots of divorcees on the market. So why did she feel like an old lady playing teenager again?

She'd just checked her reflection in the floor length mirror beside the front door for the twentieth time when she heard his car door slam. Suddenly, she didn't want to go anywhere with Joel. She didn't even want to see him again. Her palms were clammy; her heart a solid lump of stone weighing heavy in her chest. She should have called and canceled. Every nerve in her body wanted to run back up to her sanctuary and refuse to answer the door. But adult women didn't act like that, so Stella sucked up her fears and opened the door when he knocked.

He leaned against the screen door with that same bold, cocky grin she remembered from all those years ago. Although a little older, every nuance exuding from Joel told Stella that he hadn't changed one bit. A divorce hadn't made a man out of him and she'd bet dollars to donuts that by the time the evening ended, he'd join the ranks of the rest of the men unfit for anything but a twenty-two bullet.

"I'll grab my coat and then I'm ready," she said quickly so he wouldn't even take one step inside the door.

Rance was the only boarder that night. Supper had been served and he was in his room. She hadn't told him she was going out, but that wasn't any of his business. After all he was a customer, not a boyfriend.

Joel opened the car door for her. "You haven't changed much."

She laughed, nervously. Maybe she was wrong about Joel. Just maybe he wasn't a braggart and blow hard anymore. Perhaps he was as bewildered with his recent divorce as she was. "You have. You don't have a baby face anymore. And you've got enough beard that you probably have to shave at least twice a week instead of twice a month. Remember that beard you tried to grow and you ended up looking like the fellow on Scooby Doo?"

He started the engine of his low slung bright red sports car. "Hey, now! Five years is enough to grow a man out of a boy. You just got more beautiful."

"Thank you, but flattery will get you nowhere with me. But then you always were a charmer."

"Never could charm you enough though,

could I?"

It wasn't there. That breathlessness she felt when she first knew Mitch, or even when Rance touched her fingertips. It just wasn't there, which was probably a good thing. That kind of relationship only ended in heart ache. It burned itself out and there wasn't anything left but cold ashes.

He laid his hand on her knee where bare skin showed at the top of the boots and began to inch his fingers upward and inward. "Penny for your thoughts."

She picked his hand up and laid it back on the arm rest between them. "My thoughts aren't for sale."

He reached across the arm rest and deliberately let his hand rest on her thigh. "Hey, Stella, we're adults, now. We're not kids and we've both been married. Don't be prudish, honey."

She pushed his hand away. "Don't be so pushy — honey."

"Whew, some leopards never change their spots." He whistled through his teeth.

"Not this one. So we're going to Braums for ice cream. Do they still make a mean banana split?" She changed the subject. She was going to enjoy herself this evening if it caused a snowstorm right in the devil's backyard.

He drove south on the two lane highway toward Dickson. "They do. Now tell me about your divorce. Is it true he just came in one day and tossed you out?"

"More or less. Let's talk about you." She changed the subject again.

"Okay," he agreed too quickly. "I got married, had two daughters and got a divorce last month. It will be final in about five more and then I'm a free man."

"Short and sweet," she said. Talk about changing a leopard's spots. Most of the time the years just aged a person into a more condensed version of what they'd been all their lives. And if anyone got out the dictionary and looked up the word ego they'd probably find Joel's picture right beside it. It oozed out his pores as much as that overpowering shaving lotion which made her nose twitch. He should switch to something less offensive. Something more like Rance used.

He turned west in the little town of Dickson and drove toward Ardmore. "Want the gory details? She was cold as ice and I went hunting for warmth. When I found it she tossed me out and filed for divorce. Said she wouldn't stay married to someone she couldn't trust. But it wasn't my fault. She was too cold for any man."

"Enough gory details." Stella dreaded the next few hours.

The hot fudge sundae was the best she'd eaten in ages. The evening was the longest she'd spent in her entire lifetime. When they started home, he opted for I-35, right up the interstate rather than going back through Dickson. He drove through Davis and Sulphur, then south through the Chickasaw National Recreation Area, simply known as 'the park' to the local residents. She'd wondered at him going ten miles further than necessary, but understood his reasoning when he kept suggesting they pull over into one of the many side roads to have a look at the night life.

"Joel, we're not in high school. I don't want to go parking with you. I barely know you anymore and we've both been through a lot, so let's don't rush things," she said bluntly.

"Marriage didn't make you any less a prude, did it?"

"And it didn't make you any less a jerk, did it?"

"Come on, Stella. Have a heart," he said.

"Grow up," she told him.

"Well, here we are. Back home. Can I come inside?" He acted as if she hadn't just insulted him.

"No and don't bother walking me to the door."

"I'm a gentleman, Stella."

She opened the door and he grabbed her in a fierce hug, pressing his lips to hers. She kept her eyes wide open and felt more like her lips had been molested than been kissed passionately.

"Why don't I sneak in for a while? You didn't mean those barbs. You're just scared of a relationship but you are definitely right about one thing. We don't need to park along the side of the road at our age. Not when there's a whole inn full of waiting beds," he whispered in her ear.

"I don't think so." Her nose began to twitch and she tried ward off the inevitable. "Aaaachooo!"

Stella never could sneeze like a lady and the sneeze exploded like it came from a two hundred fifty pound mountain man. She apologized, wiping at his jacket, trying to cover her nose as it began to tickle again, and fighting back laughter at the look on his face. It wasn't easy balancing all three especially with him stumbling backward down the porch steps.

"Yuck. Well, I'll call next week." He threw over his shoulder, snarling his nose and making fast tracks toward his vehicle.

A simple sneeze. She'd have to remember to carry a vial of black pepper in her purse from now on when she dated. She yelled across the yard. "Thanks for the ice cream and conversation. But Joel, don't call me. It didn't work then and it's not going to work now. We just don't mix."

"We'll see," he gave her his best grin which usually made round heels on all the women he knew. One smile and they'd fall backwards on the nearest bed, sand bar or even railroad track and pull him right down with them.

There wouldn't be any we'll sees. He could call every night until three days past eternity and she still wouldn't be interested in providing warmth for Joel. He hadn't grown from a boy into a man. He didn't know anything about a lasting commitment. All he was interested in was a moment of instant gratification. She opened the door and went inside, didn't bother to turn on the light and headed up the stairs.

"Dang you, Rance," she swore under her breath. "Until you invaded my house, I was doing just fine."

Rance came out of the kitchen. He wore flannel pajama bottoms and no shirt or shoes. He had a chest full of dark, soft looking hair and carried a cup of coffee. "Did I hear my name mentioned?"

She wanted to take the coffee from him and drink it all just to get the taste of Joel's kiss out of her mouth, but she wanted to lay her face against his chest even more.

"Yes, you did," she covered her error swiftly. "I was muttering about what I should prepare for your breakfast."

He sipped the steaming coffee. "Waffles?"

"Then waffles it will be," she said.

"Where did you go? Out on a date? You're all dressed up."

"That is none of your business," she said.

"What's his name?"

"I said that's none of your business. Good night, Rance." She left him standing there staring at her.

CHAPTER THREE

Rance hung around the kitchen while Stella loaded the dishwasher. Another family occupied all the rooms but his. They were only there for breakfast and didn't arrive back until bedtime so it had been only Rance and Stella at the dinner table.

"Come sit with me in the living room when you finish."

She shook her head. "That isn't part of the contract. Breakfast from six to seven on the bar or until eight if the clients arise a little later, no lunch, supper promptly at six, family style at the table, and BYOE, that's bring your own entertainment."

"But," he frowned. "Stella, just what is it that makes you so distant? I'm just asking you to sit with me and have a little adult conversation. It's been a long day and I've worked hard."

"Oh, yeah, what did you do? Sit in a deer stand or behind a tree waiting for Bambi to

57

poke his little head up so you could shoot him. Sounds like hard work to me, all right," she said.

"I was only hunting that first weekend, Stella. I've been busy on my house the rest of this week. I bought the property right next door to you and have been working on it before the movers and the hired help come up from Waco. The painters were there on Monday. The cabinets were installed yesterday. The plumbers and electricians have worked both days. Carpet came today and tomorrow the moving vans will be here. On Friday the cattle trucks will arrive with the livestock."

"Then you'll be leaving early?" She asked, amazed that she could speak. Good grief, the man would be living in the old Morgan place right next door to her five acres. Instead of disappearing, not to be heard of again at least until next hunting season, he'd be right there, a quarter of a mile away. Did he get his two children every other weekend and summers? Would his ex-wife bring the children?

He leaned over the counter. "Oh, no, that's why I rented a room for extra time. I need to unpack and take care of things. I'll need every single day I've got booked. Come in the living room and talk to me?

We are going to be neighbors so we might as well get to know each other. Tell me why a beautiful, young woman like you has strapped herself to a twenty four hour, seven day a week job?"

She was speechless for several seconds, trying to collect her thoughts into an intelligent answer or comment, but nothing floated from the heavens. While she was deciding how in the world she was going to refuse, the door bell rang.

Saved by the bell.

She hurried to open the door only to find the devil wearing tight jeans and a smile on the other side.

Joel leaned against the jamb, one hip cocked to keep the screen door open and his foot already preventing her closing the other door in his face. "Hello, gorgeous. How about an ice cream at Braums or a long ride in the country?"

"I'm busy tonight, Joel. I told you last week this wouldn't work. Sorry you drove all the way out here for nothing," Stella said.

He hooked an arm out and pulled her toward him in one fluid motion. "Oh, darlin', it ain't for nothin'."

When she was chest to chest with him, his lips already puckered and leaning forward to kiss her, she put her hands on his shoul-

59

ders and pushed backward. "I said I'm busy," she said in an icy tone as she stumbled.

Rance grabbed her around the waist to keep her from falling. "Whoa, there, honey. Who's here? Do we have company?"

Joel shoved his way into the living room. He drew his eyebrows down into a frown. "Who's this? Does he know we are an item?"

"I'm Rance Harper, Stella's new neighbor. She sure didn't tell me you two were an item. If I'd known, I wouldn't have bought the old Morgan ranch. Here I thought she was only seeing me," Rance's eyes glittered in amusement.

Joel glared at her. "Looks like she's been two-timing us both. So, Stella?"

"So what?" She removed Rance's hands. His touch caused her heart to do acrobatics. Joel's touch turned her stomach.

"So which one is it? Surely, you aren't going to give me up for this wannabe rancher."

"Ah, it pains me to do so but I'm afraid I must," Stella felt like a second grader on the playground. Adults didn't act like this, but then no one had ever accused Joel of maturity. Women seldom admit their age. Men never act theirs.

"You're saying you are choosing him over me?" Joel asked incredulously.

"That's it. I'm saying that. Yes, I'd choose Rance over you. Now please leave."

"You are a fool. You didn't know how to get a man when you were young. Didn't know how to keep the one you got and don't know which one would give you a good time now. Good-bye, Stella," Joel said dramatically and slammed the door on his way out.

"You are welcome," Rance said.

"I don't have to thank you, Rance. I could have handled it on my own so there's no thanks due. When a slug crawls up in the kitchen you just pour salt on it and it'll melt. I could have salted Joel down without your help. And this is all so sophomoric — it's pitiful."

"Yeah, but it was fun. Admit it. And was that a bitter history I heard?"

"Could be but it's none of your business," she nodded.

"Oh, yes it is. I've just saved you from a fate worse than death, and to pay me back you can have coffee with me in the living room."

"Joel is a fate worse than death but the answer is no."

Rance followed her to the kitchen. "But you chose me over him."

"I'd choose a snuff dipping mentally chal-

61

lenged idiot over Joel," she snapped at him.

Rance threw back his head and roared. He felt more alive than he had in years.

She shook a stack of coffee filters at him. "Don't you laugh at me."

"Why? That was funny. I could visualize you with this big ox of a dummy with snuff in the corners of his mouth and wearing bibbed overalls so dirty that they could stand in the corner by themselves. Does lover boy Joel know that he's taking a back seat to that vision?"

"I don't give a tiny rat's rump what he knows or doesn't know," she said, a smile tickling the corner of her mouth. "Okay, okay, you win. A cup of coffee in the living room but only fifteen minutes worth of adult conversation."

And you'll sit on one end of the sofa and I'll take the chair as far away as possible. Nothing can go wrong if we keep a room between us and a cup of coffee in our hands. Lord, why do I have to be attracted to dark haired, dark eyed men? It's not fair. Why can't some good old boy make my little heart flutter?

She carried a cup in each hand to the living room only to find Rance on his hands and knees, his face close to the floor.

She set the coffee on an end table. "What are you doing?"

"Lost a contact," he said.

She squatted beside him and began to look in the same area.

He held up something on the end of his finger. "Ah, here it is, but ruined. Must have stepped on it and ground it into the carpet."

Their eyes met, not six inches apart, over the tip of a finger where a dark brown mangled piece of plastic stuck.

"You're not brown eyed," she was taken aback.

"No, they are blue," he said.

"Well, how about that?" She smiled.

He removed the other lens. "Hey, if I'd known you'd smile over blue eyes instead of brown, I'd have lost both of them. You look all out of focus with one lens in and one out. I'm blind without them so that means you'd better sit on the sofa with me or you'll just be a voice coming across the room instead of the lady I'm talking to."

She hugged the far end of the sofa, wedging herself close to the arm. "So why are you wearing brown contacts?"

"Because my ex-wife hated brown eyed men. It's a mental thing according to my therapist. He says that having brown eyes gives me the power to keep her away," Rance only squinted a little when he looked at Stella.

"You have a therapist?"

"Sure, doesn't everyone this day and age? I told my grandpa that I should've given up ranching and studied to be one. It pays much, much better."

Stella looked at the clock sitting on the mantle above the fireplace. "So what do you want to talk about? Your fifteen minutes are running out."

Stella was slightly out of focus. Even with her make-up worn off and blond hair tied back in a pony tail at the nape of her neck, she was still lovely, even if a little fuzzy around the edges.

"What's a lovely lady like you doing in a place like this?" He used the age-old bar line.

"I told you before. Granny left the Inn to me when she died. My marriage was already on the rocks and had been for months. When my ex found out I couldn't sell the place for upteen years it was the last straw. Evidently while I was working to support his wannabe acting career, he was sleeping with his agent. A few weeks after Granny died, he came home with a song and dance routine common to a lot of actors or at least those who want to be on the cover of tabloids. I was a hindrance to his career. Simple as that. I came home, opened up

64

shop and started cleaning and cooking. Next question?"

He slid down the leather sofa until she was in complete focus. "No more questions," he said softly.

"Then we sit here in comfortable silence until the clock strikes ten thirty or have you been paid in full for your intervention with Joel Lucifer?"

Rance grinned. "That's not really his name is it?"

"No, but I expect he was spawned by the devil and it's his secret name," she said.

"What's your biggest fear?" He asked out of the clear blue.

"The 'C' word. I'm terrified of commitment," she said without hesitation. "And yours?"

"The same. I'm not ever getting married again. I might have a fling or two. I might have a life long lady partner who shares my life but I got stung too bad the first time to try it again. Julie was her name. She was a tall blond with dark brown eyes. She flat out broke me from sucking eggs, I'm here to tell you."

"Not me. I want to get married. I want one of those lifetime things. I want the marriage license. I want to fight and make up, have a yard full of kids, and someday have someone to hold my hand when I'm taking my last breath and tell me to walk slowly because it won't be long until they're following me. I want all that, but I'm terrified of making a commitment to get it," she said.

"You could have every bit of it without a cursed marriage license, then you'd be free to walk away any time without problems," he said.

"Not me. If I'm going to have a lifetime thing, it's going to be with all the bells and whistles," she turned to see his expression, only to find his face six inches away and leaning in. The last thing she remembered before his lips found hers was that he had the longest eyelashes she'd ever seen on a man.

His soft, full lips knew exactly how to create a steamy, warm feeling in the pit of her stomach. Time stood still. The earth stopped moving. Sensations flooded Stella that she hadn't felt in a long time, if ever. She'd kissed her first boyfriend back when she was in the ninth grade and there'd been too many to count since then. But even Mitch, with all his good looks and finesse hadn't affected her like Rance. She wanted to pull away and run to the safety of her bedroom, but she had no power over her body. She wrapped her arms around his neck and when the kiss ended and another began, she melted into him.

An hour later, her lips were bee-stung swollen, her heart pounded, her body wanted what it couldn't have and she felt so foolish she blushed crimson. She pulled away and stood to her feet, her knees more than a little weak and her conscience telling her that she was a grown woman, not a high school student who made out with her boyfriend on the sofa.

"I think it's time for . . ." She stammered.

"Bed? Your place or mine?"

"Neither, Rance, and you know it. You want a lady companion. I want a lifetime thing. We'd both be wasting our time. Besides, I don't take this kind of thing casually. This should have never happened. I have a rule about not getting involved with customers."

"But I won't always be a customer. I'll soon be a neighbor and besides, I know what kind of woman you are, Stella. I was teasing. I would like to see you sometime. I'll be moving into my house in a few days but I'd like to take you to dinner or see a movie or go to Dallas for a play," he picked up his cup and carried it to the kitchen. Usually a session like he'd just enjoyed netted more benefits. Maybe eventually Stella would come around to his way of thinking. The geography was perfect: living right next door to each other but with enough space between them to keep it from being too close. It could be a lifelong arrangement with no permanent ties. Lifelong; not lifetime.

"I don't think so, Rance. It would be totally unprofitable. Good night." She left her cup on the end table and headed for the stairs, forcing boneless legs to carry her up to her bedroom where she shut the door and flopped down on her bed.

Her body was in a whirlwind of swirling unfulfilled passion. She had one steadfast rule she'd never broken, no matter what, and that was she did not get involved with her boarders. She'd just shattered that statute into a million jagged pieces but it wouldn't happen again.

She touched her swollen lips and felt her warm cheeks. The right man to make her swoon, the right distance between them once he moved, the handsome good looks with one minor blind flaw, everything perfect . . . except he wanted a mistress and she wanted to be a mother with legitimate children. Rance already had his two kids and she had none. She could be a mother to step children without a problem, but she wanted her own to go with them.

Now isn't that a hoot and just as adolescent as necking on the sofa for an hour? Rance told me what he wanted and he asked me for a date. He certainly did not ask me to be that mistress he was talking about. I've jumped to conclusions just like a kid would do.

She eased off the bed and switched on the light, went to the bathroom and stared at her reflection in the mirror. The same Stella looked back at her that had awakened that morning. "I am an adult — I will behave as one from now on," she removed the last dregs of her makeup and washed her face. "This was a lapse in judgment and will never happen again. Lord, I hate to face him at breakfast after that little episode, but it'll have to be done."

She turned on water in the shower and dropped her jeans and shirt on the floor. Tomorrow was another day, as Scarlett had said in *Gone With The Wind.* Stella would pretend nothing had happened when Rance came to the breakfast table. He'd probably be just as anxious to avoid things as she would, and if he did ask for a date she was going to refuse him. The man had more power over her than she was willing to deal with.

She awoke the next morning at five

o'clock. There was nothing left of the night before but a guilty conscience and the faint whiff of his cologne on her shirt when she picked it up from the bathroom floor. She dreaded going downstairs to pretend the whole night had meant nothing because she was a terrible actress.

Rance had spent a sleepless night. He was sitting in the living room when he heard the tell-tale squeak as she stepped on the fifth stair step at a few minutes past five. Nothing had prepared him for the way he felt when his lips met hers in those earth shattering kisses. It was as if two souls had met after three lifetimes of drifting around in eternity. The search had ended and they'd found their mates, two ex-spouses too late.

He'd meant to give her a few minutes in the kitchen then slip in there before the rest of the house was up and moving. He'd pretend as if it were any other morning and he wanted a cup of coffee before breakfast was served. Why couldn't he swallow his pride and admit she'd gotten under his skin and squirmed into his heart?

Because every time I look at her I'll be reminded that Julie broke that same heart and I can't trust women.

They arrived in the kitchen at the same time. Rance raised an eyebrow in her direction, but she ignored it. Her legs trembled and heart fluttered but she wasn't making the same mistake twice. Burn me once, shame on you; burn me twice, shame on me.

Rance cleared his throat. "Good mornin'. Are we having pancakes?" He watched her put the iron grill on the stove, taking up two burners.

"Yes, it's Granny's old recipe," she said.

Rance wanted to bypass the pancakes and spend another hour on the couch, then go on to the bedroom, leaving a trail of clothing down the long hallway or up the steps. But that wasn't going to happen. Stella might be a divorced woman but the old adages about divorcees being hot to trot didn't apply to her. She was a lady. What was it she'd said? She wanted a lifetime thing. Well, Rance was fresh out of lifetime things to offer. At one time in his life he'd had one but he'd given it to the wrong woman.

He watched her pour perfect circles on the griddle. "Granny Brannon was a very wonderful lady."

"A very wise one, too," Stella said. "I hope someday my granddaughter will say the same thing about me."

"I'm sure she will," Rance turned and went to look at the squirrels scampering through the pecan trees in the back yard. They had not a care in the world. It didn't matter that winter was on the way. They ate. They slept. They played. He'd take a lesson from them. He'd live simply in Murray County, Oklahoma and he wouldn't let his next door neighbor affect him any more.

CHAPTER FOUR

Rance opened his eyes and stared blankly at the ceiling, a lady curled up in the crook of his right arm and another one at his feet. His wondered if Stella was up and making breakfast yet. He sighed deeply and wondered why it seemed like every waking thought involved Stella. Especially since the night they'd shared all those passionate kisses. Why couldn't he be content to live with his ladies, his babies as the fellows called them, and put the tall, blond inn owner out of his mind?

He pushed the big, orange cat off his arm and nudged the black and white one away from his feet. "Okay, ladies, it's time to rise and shine. I don't care if you are more bear than feline at the crack of dawn, it's Saturday morning and we've got business to take care of."

He dressed casually in jeans and a red polo shirt. His desk top looked like a tornado and a hurricane had a wrestling match in the middle of it. He sighed as he looked at the paper work on his desk. Vowing it would be organized by the end of the day, he picked up the first piece. He would categorize it all into several manageable stacks which his secretary could take care of first thing on Monday morning. He managed to get it half done before he threw up his hands and walked out the back door. An icy breeze chilled him. The hired hands were already out around the horse stables. A fleeting image passed in front of his eyes. He'd hadn't seen Stella since he'd checked out of Brannon Inn the week before but there she was, a vision with her long blond hair tied back in a pony tail.

"Well, damn it anyway," he clenched his hands into fists.

He opened the door to the barn to the drone of a dozen men all talking amongst themselves about the days work. They'd all brought their families and moved from Texas to Oklahoma with him. Some resided in Sulphur, a few in Davis, and one in Mill Creek. When he'd approached them about selling out in Waco and moving to a small southern Oklahoma town most of his staff had agreed to relocate. It made his job easier because he didn't have to retrain the help and besides most of them were friends. When they noticed him the noise stopped. Before he could say a word, his cell phone set up a howl in his shirt pocket. He answered it and they went back to their conversation.

"Well, my, my, did I catch you at a bad time?" A feminine voice asked.

"Yes, you did. Who is this?" He asked bluntly. It wasn't Julie, his ex-wife. She had the gravely voice of a long time smoker. A bit sexy, but not like this high pitched, upbeat woman on the other end of the line. It sure wasn't Stella. He'd know that voice anywhere. At midnight with his eyes shut. In broad daylight in the middle of a busy shopping mall. It was sweet fire.

"This is Jewel Carpenter. You might not remember me. A few weeks ago we shared a few meals at a little bed and breakfast in Sulphur, Oklahoma," she said, jogging his memory back to a dark haired pixie lady who liked to take long hikes in the woods.

"Of course, I remember you. I just didn't recognize your voice." He said.

"Well, we're in Davis for the weekend, and . . ." she waited.

"And?" He said.

"I'm not used to asking outright for a good-looking man to take me to dinner," she said. "But I can do it. Are you busy tonight?"

"No. I mean, yes, I do have plans. I thought you and your family was going to the Ouachita Mountains and how did you get my cell phone number?"

"We are but not this weekend. We had such a good time in the Arbuckles we decided to give it another try before our other trip. You really were paying attention that night. I got your cell phone number from the register at the inn before we left. I'm very resourceful. We were going to stay with Mrs. Barnum but she is going away this weekend. We sure had a good time that weekend didn't we?"

Anger rose up like a thunderstorm inside Rance. *"Brannon!"*

"No bantered. Remember, you said you couldn't live without steak and we were eating spinach lasagna. Miss Barnum did make a good meal, but most women her age know how to cook."

He clenched his teeth. "Brannon. Not Barnum. Stella's name is *Brannon!*"

"Well, pardooooon me! So what have you got going with Miss . . . Bran-non?" She stressed both syllables of the name. "How did you two get on first name basis?"

"That's none of your business, Jewel.

Sorry, I'm busy tonight."

"Where are you going? To Dallas with her?" Jewel asked rudely.

"That, too, is none of your business."

"Well, can't blame a girl for trying. Go have a good time with the old lady in the fancy Wyndham Hotel. Maybe you'll even go to the Travis Tritt concert with her. I wouldn't waste my time on a country music singer. While you're there with Mrs. Brantham, remember the young woman you passed up. I hope you can't get me out of your mind. Good-bye, Rance," she said in her sexiest voice.

"Good-bye," he said.

And thank you Jewel.

A grin teased the corners of his mouth and his eyes twinkled. He picked up the phone again and dialed the hotel in Dallas. The manager said they certainly could put Mr. Harper in a room for the weekend.

He walked over to the men waiting for the day's instructions. "Hey, do the minimum chores this weekend and go home. Half can do morning duties. The rest can take care of the evening ones. Or divide them by Saturday and Sunday if you want a whole day with your families. I'm going to be out of pocket tomorrow and Sunday."

An hour later, Rance pulled on a pair of

tight, crisply starched jeans and a white western shirt. The cats were busy batting a toy around under the bed and didn't offer an opinion on how he looked. He'd heard that folks own dogs but merely feed cats. Maybe that was why he liked them so well. They were independent, granting him the favor of rubbing their soft fur when it suited them, and demanding nothing from him but a warm body to sleep next to and a full dish of cat food. It was hard to believe they were really female.

He checked his reflection in the mirror. He was crazy. Stella would take one look at him and tell him to drop dead. What they had that night was just the by-product of her anger toward that creepy Joel. It had nothing to do with him. Any man would have filled the bill just as well. So why was he hauling a suitcase and his boot bag out to the truck? She didn't want him and he wasn't about to get serious about a woman. Not after Julie. Not after the pain that broke his old cowboy heart in half.

I need a vacation. I've been working hard for two solid weeks. We've got things up and running and the plans drawn up to put hired help houses on the property by spring. The place can run itself for two days. He argued with his conscience.

Stella picked up a leather suitcase and matching garment bag and made her way to one of the bedrooms just off the sitting room. "Wow, this suite is downright fancy. Okay if I have this bedroom?"

"Hey, it's fine with me. I've stayed here lots of times and I don't plan to spend much time in this suite anyway." Tina hauled her suitcase into the other bedroom.

Stella sat on the end of the bed and soaked up the atmosphere. If she didn't see a single show, dance even one two-step, or eat anywhere but in the closest McDonald's, it would be fine with her. Just getting away from Murray County for a couple of days was sheer heaven. If only Rance could be beside her.

"Now where in the hell did that come from," she mumbled.

"What?" Tina asked from the doorway.

"Just thinking aloud," Stella answered.

"Well, let's go shop. I'll change and we'll unpack later. I'll call a cab to take us to the Galleria. I've got reservations already made for lunch at The Grill on the Alley, then we'll shop some more and go see if Travis Tritt fills out his jeans as well as he did when we were in high school."

"Wow, you've really got us all mapped out. I thought we'd just eat at the restaurant in the hotel and play catch up on the gossip while we swim in the indoor pool."

"Not this time, lady. Can't find any of those sweet talkin' devils from around these parts in the hotel. We're on the prowl and we're lookin' for a rich imported tom cat for you. We don't want a good ole boy from Oklahoma or even northern Texas. Nope, we're off to shop and eat in the fancy lunch place. Besides, I have an ulterior motive. That's where the pretty cowboy I told you about works. He's a waiter there and his name is Brock."

Stella whistled through her teeth. "Surely you're kiddin' me about a waiter. For crying out loud girl, you are a famous actress now. You've hit the big time with that last movie. Lord, girl, I wouldn't be surprised if you don't get some kind of award for your part."

"I'll be back in a minute," Tina smiled. "You get ready for a day on the town."

Tina had changed into a pair of tight black jeans, a red western blouse with a cut out neckline and lace up Roper boots when she came back. "An award would be great but Brock is even better. I met him in Holly-

80

wood when he was taking a year off school and thinking about acting. He didn't like the ups and downs, so he's working as a waiter while he finishes up his last year of college."

Stella pulled her hair back and secured it with a wide clip. "I can't believe you came to Dallas for a weekend fling with some wannabe actor you picked up in Hollywood. Your mother would drop with a heart attack if she knew that."

"Don't be naive, Stella. I didn't pick him up. I let him pick me up and I dang sure didn't forget him. I may never forget him. But I couldn't have a lifetime of something that intense. It would kill me dead in six weeks. You don't look so bad yourself, girlfriend. I may have to take a back seat to you tonight. Look out Dallas here we come. But first we'll take a stroll through the mall and maybe even buy a few things, like good little tourists should, so you can tell your momma and Maggie all about it. I'll take Mother a new outfit and she'll never know I'm here to meet Brock. She wouldn't have a heart attack if she knew what I really do when I fly into Dallas and stay a couple of days before I go home, but she'd probably drop down on her knees and pray for my erring soul until we all hear Gabriel's horn signaling the rapture."

Stella shook her head. She wondered what Rance would think if he knew she was in Dallas and 'on the prowl.'

She scolded herself as they waited for the elevator. *Damn it, I didn't plan an impromptu get-away with Tina and spend mega-bucks so I could conjure up visions of Rance.*

Tina had been in the class below her at Sulphur High School and part of the reason Mitch made his earth shattering decision to quit college and go to Hollywood. If a small town girl who had crooked front teeth and carrot red hair could make it big in the movie industry, it was a cinch that someone as handsome as Mitch could have any part he wanted.

Two days before Tina had called and asked Stella to join her in Dallas for a weekend of fun and then drive her home for a two week visit with her mother. At first Stella said she was too busy. Her sister, Maggie, and niece, Lauren, were coming from Coffeyville, Kansas and she planned to spend time with them. But Tina twisted her arm, slightly, and Stella agreed quickly.

"Okay, lead the way," Stella stepped out of the elevator and toward the hotel's front door.

Tina pushed through the doors and

headed toward a waiting cab. "Look out Dallas. Here we come!"

Tina prattled like a tourist guide as they wandered through the mall. "And now we have Gucci. Do we want a new purse or shoes? Notice please that purses are on sale at fifty percent off in this pre-Christmas sale and my mother would probably love one. She can use it to carry her money to the church and pay the preacher to spend hours praying for my wayward soul."

Stella laughed. Tina was a positive, upbeat friend and she was glad they'd decided on the spur of the moment to take the trip. "Oh, Tina, you are awful."

"Yes, I am. I'm going inside to buy the purse. Did you know that this mall was featured in *The Devil Wears Prada*? I wanted that part but somehow my agent couldn't even get me an audition and today I don't give a dang because I'm going to see Brock."

"Methinks maybe Brock is the devil the way he makes your eyes shine," Stella teased as they looked through the purse display.

"He could be. You know that old saying 'the devil made me do it'? Hey, what do you think the devil really wears?"

Stella answered before she thought. "Blue jeans and brown contacts."

"Aha, I hear a story," Tina stopped.

"One that's already ended so it doesn't bear repeating. How long has it been since you saw Brock?" Stella changed the subject.

"Six months and that's too long," Tina said.

"You said you couldn't take a lifetime of something as intense as Brock, so why are you going to see him again? Aren't you just setting yourself up for a bad heart ache?"

"I can't take a lifetime, but I can take two days at a time."

They shopped the rest of the morning and went to the restaurant at exactly noon. Tina had made reservations just as she'd promised so they didn't have to wait in line. The minute they were seated a tall handsome man strutted over to their table, raised a heavy dark eyebrow and laid his hand on Tina's shoulder. "Well, well, look what the Hollywood wind blew over here."

"And look who is still trying to get through med school." Tina bantered right back and reached up to touch his hand.

"What would you like to do tonight?"

"We're doing the Travis Tritt concert. Want to go with us?"

He sized Stella up and down. "Can I bring my room mate to entertain your friend?"

Stella promptly kicked Tina under the table.

"No, she's already got plans," Tina said.

"Then let me take your order ladies and I'll see you after the concert. I've got some studying to do so I'd better have business before pleasure." Brock whipped out a pen.

"Good looking." Stella murmured when he was out of hearing range. "And he actually made you blush."

"If you had the memories I've got, you'd blush, too." Tina admitted. "Hey, you look a little red around the cheeks yourself. What are you hiding?"

"Not one thing," Stella lied. "Sounds like you are bit bad."

"Yes, I am. But not to the point of stupidity. At least not yet."

They were thirty minutes late to the concert and arrived among stares and wolf whistles with a few recognizing Tina and begging for autographs. A short, feisty red head and a tall blond, both in tight blue jeans drew attention like honey draws bees, and before they'd been there five minutes a cowboy was sitting beside Stella. He was tall, had the prettiest blond hair, feathered back just perfectly, wore his jeans bunched up over his boot tops, and a grin that said he liked what he saw beside him.

"Name is Hank, but not Williams. Where ya'll from, ma'am." He drawled in true

Texas fashion.

"My name is Stella Brannon. I'm from Sulphur, Oklahoma."

"Small world, Stella. I'm from Denison, Texas. I'm going to be rich and famous someday. I'm here to see if I can get an interview with Travis and pass along some demo tapes of songs I've written for him. What's your business in Dallas?" He slipped an arm around her.

No fireworks exploded. The man was Mitch's opposite. Blond. Handsome in a rugged way. But his touch on her arm did nothing but make her want to slap him.

"Just trying to relax and get away from southern Oklahoma for a weekend." She admitted honestly.

"Well, I'm just the fellow to help a fine lady like you relax," he said.

He was much too cocky for Stella's taste. *Why is it that blond haired men just can't make my heart flutter.*

No answers bounced off the walls of the concert hall

"Married?" he asked.

She shook her head. "Divorced."

"Me, too. Want to talk about it?"

She shook her head. "Not at all."

"Me, either. Woman didn't want me to write songs. Expected me to work at the car dealership for the rest of my life and never pursue my dreams. Said a man with a wife, a house payment and two kids ought to settle down and grow up. Hell, I ain't never going to grow up. I'm going to follow bands and when I'm walking up that aisle at the CMA Awards someday to get the award for the best songwriter, she's going to know just what she threw away."

Stella tried to smile but it came out more a grimace. Why did she attract men like Hank and Joel? All she wanted was a nice, quiet lifestyle with someone who truly loved her. Someone to spend the rest of her days with, to sit on the porch in a rocking chair when life was ebbing away and to hold her hand while she made the transition from a living being to a spiritual one.

"I'm going for a beer. Want one?" Hank asked.

"No thanks," she said.

Travis had performed for fifteen minutes non stop when he slung his guitar over his back and said, "Little surprise while I'm taking a break. Everyone give it up for Sara Evans who'll entertain you for a few minutes." Sara stepped up to the mike and sang one of her old songs, "Born to Fly."

As she listened to the words, Stella wondered if her time had come to fly. Fly away from all the chains she'd wrapped around her heart when she and Mitch divorced. Soar up away from the bitter taste in her soul. Someone tapped her on the shoulder. For a split second she thought she smelled Rance's cologne.

"Excuse me? Anyone sitting here?" He asked.

She looked up to see Rance. Right there in Dallas. Anger boiled up from the pit of her soul and engulfed her in so much rage her face was scarlet. How dare he follow her.

"What are you doing here?" She gasped.

"I'm in Dallas to look at a bull tomorrow afternoon. Heard Travis was singing tonight. Called him and he said to come on to the concert and we'd visit afterwards. Imagine my surprise when I saw you. What are you doing here?"

"I'm on a much deserved mini-vacation," she said shortly.

"Come with that fellow who just left?" He asked.

"No, never met him before."

"Going home with him?"

"That isn't a bit of your business," she said.

"Where you staying?"

"At the Econolodge." She lied.

"Who is that?" Tina whispered when Rance had settled into the seat beside Stella.

"It's the devil in tight jeans and brown contacts," Stella whispered back. "Who claims to know Travis personally."

"Handsome devil," Tina grinned then reached for her cell phone that had vibrated in her pocket. The smile grew the longer she listened.

"Brock is finished early and meeting me at the hotel. I'll see you in the morning. Got a way home?"

Stella waved her away. "I know how to hail a cab."

"Who is that?" Rance asked.

"My friend from California. Well, she's originally from Sulphur but she went to Hollywood and is an actress now."

"Where's she going? Is that Tina McIvey?"

"Yes, it is and she's going back to the hotel to answer both of your questions."

"I can give you a ride when the show is over. My truck is just outside," Rance said.

"And miss the back stage party with Travis. I couldn't let you do that," she said sarcastically.

"We'll make an appearance at the party and then I'll take you home," he said.

Great balls of fire, he wasn't joking or lying about the party. He really did know Travis. Wait until she went home and told Lauren that she'd actually seen the man in person, not just up on the stage.

"All right," she nodded, still not believing him. How would a rancher know Travis Tritt?

Every time his hand brushed against hers on the arm rest she shivered. She could feel his piercing eyes when they glanced her way. Travis sang. She fought the urge to squirm. Travis sang some more. She wished she was home in the safety of her rut. Travis ended the concert with "T-R-O-U-B-L-E." She felt like she was wallowing in trouble just sitting beside Rance.

They made their way to the center aisle and slowly down to the stage. Rance put his hand on the small of her back to guide her, heating up every fiber in her body. When was this deception going to end? Surely the guards wouldn't just let him walk backstage with no pass or anything. What kind of tall tale would he spin then?

The guard shook hands with Rance. "Well, hello Rance. How's things going? Heard you sold out in Waco and bought a place in southern Oklahoma. Who you going to root for when Texas plays OU now?"

"The Longhorns. I'm still a Texan even if I have crossed the river," Rance said. "This is Stella Brannon, my neighbor in Oklahoma. She's probably going to yell for the Sooners. Will that keep her from going back stage with me?"

"Not if she promises to keep that information under her hat. Don't guess she's got an OU sweatshirt hiding in her boots, does she?"

Stella shook her head. "No, I do not."

"Well, then go on back and visit with Travis. He'll be right happy to see you."

"Thanks, Willy," Rance said.

"Willy?" Stella asked when they were out of hearing distance.

"Not Willy, the great, just Willy one of the stage hands. He went to school with me down in Waco. If Texas hadn't beat OU this year, you might have been barred from going with me."

"He looks big enough to play for the Longhorns," Stella said.

Rance wrapped an arm around her waist, claiming his rights even if only for a little while. "He is, but blew out his knee in the last game of our senior year. Was a helluva line backer. Ah, here we are."

She met Travis and the three of them visited for fifteen minutes, with Rance doing most of the talking, telling about his ranch in Oklahoma and inviting Travis to come see him when he got home from the tour. Travis said he might show up on Rance's door step. When Travis was called over to another group, Rance waved and guided Stella toward the door.

"Are you ready to go?" He asked.

"I should get an autograph for Lauren," she said.

"Why? Travis shows up at my place about once a year for some rest and relaxation. Brings his family. Rides the horses. Sleeps like a log for a few days. Gets rejuvenated and all that. Next time he comes I'll invite you and Lauren over for dinner. We'll go out this door. I'm parked in the VIP section."

"Well, well, ain't you the big shot," she said.

"No, I'm not. I'm just Rance. That's what got me in trouble with my ex. She wanted a big shot. Now where is the Econolodge located?"

Oops! She'd been caught. She could have him take her to the hotel, go inside and wait until he drove away, then call a cab, but she had no idea where the Econolodge was. There was nothing to do but 'fess up.

"I'm not at the Econolodge. Tina and I are staying at the Wyndham, not far from here," she said.

He frowned. "Why'd you tell me that, then?"

"Truth?"

"Can I handle it?" He asked.

"Probably not, so I'll just plead the fifth and not answer. Where are you staying?"

"The Wyndham. It's my choice of hotels if I have to be in Dallas," he said.

She focused on his face in the darkness of the pickup. "I'm not sure I believe in this many coincidences."

"Me, either. But I do believe in fate. What's the chances of two neighbors from southern Oklahoma finding each other amongst all those people at a concert and then staying in the same hotel? That's not coincidence, it's fate."

He handed the valet the keys to his Dodge Ram truck at the front of the hotel and escorted Stella inside, his hand on her back again, burning holes through her jeans and tattooing her skin. He pushed the up button on the elevator and waited.

"Which floor?" He asked.

"Three," she answered, catching his eyes staring right into hers in the smoky mirrors inside the elevator. "Where are you?"

"Same." He whistled one of Travis's songs.

"Fate again?"

"Guess so."

It had to be fate. How else could he have known? She'd told her mother that she was going to Dallas to give Tina a ride home but that's the only person she'd mentioned her whereabouts to. Other than that snippy Jewel who'd called and insisted that she rent them a wing on a moment's notice. There was no way her mother would be talking to Rance, or Jewel either. That left only fate and/or divine intervention, and God certainly did not have that big of a sense of humor.

"Well, here we are," she said when the doors slid open.

"Which room?"

She motioned to the door across from the elevator. "Right in front of us."

"Mine is down the hall. Want to come down for a drink or a late night movie?"

It took every ounce of willpower she had to tell him no.

He leaned against the wall in front of her door. "Okay, then. Guess I've seen you safely home."

"Thanks for taking me to the after party and giving me a ride." She inserted the plastic key into the slot.

One minute she was keeping her eyes on the door, the next she looked up to see him staring intently at her. The brown contacts were gone and his eyes were their natural color, icy blue and getting closer and closer. She barely had time to snap her eyelids shut before his lips found hers.

"Rance," she said breathlessly when he reluctantly pulled away, "this won't work. I told you before. We want two different things."

"It was just a goodnight kiss, Stella. It wasn't a proposal." His tone was chilly. He wanted that kiss to be just what he said, a goodnight kiss that did nothing for him. But it wasn't.

"Then good night," she stepped into the room, a mad sitting on her shoulder so big she couldn't have knocked it off with a bull dozer. Blast him all the way to the devil anyway.

"Good night and you are welcome," he said like a true gentleman.

She spun around, holding the door with one hand, and glaring at him. "For what?"

"Welcome for the after party and the ride. What did you think I was talking about?"

"Nothing. Not one thing. Have a safe trip home and good luck with the bull. And thank you," she said, the tone still dripping with icicles.

"What?" He stopped before he said bull. He was supposed to be in Dallas looking at a bull, not at Stella. If she knew this whole affair wasn't brought on by fate, she'd really never speak to him again. "You drive carefully, too," he stammered and didn't look back as he headed toward his room.

CHAPTER FIVE

Rance showered, shaved and put on cologne. He talked to Melanie and Grace the whole time he got ready to go to Brannon Inn. He hadn't seen Stella all week, not since they'd argued at the door to her hotel room, but he found out by sneaky means that she didn't have guests this weekend. So he was going over there to ask her to go to supper with him. It would be harder to tell him no if he was standing right there on her porch.

He had to get her out of his heart and soul. It was eating away at him and yet everytime they were together, they fought. The passion in the kisses as well as the fire when they argued kept pulling him back to her. Surely she didn't feel the same or she'd be jumping the fences between their properties.

His hands were clammy and his heart raced like it did the first time he borrowed his father's truck and took Mary Lou Smith to the picture show in Lewisville. They had watched *Fast Times at Ridgemont High* and he had blushed all the way through the movie. He'd had lots of girlfriends since that day, and he'd been married for a year and divorced a little over four years now. So why in the world did his hands get all sweaty at just the thought of Stella?

He put an old John Conlee cassette in the tape player and listened to "Rose Colored Glasses." He sang along and wondered if Stella liked John Conlee as well as she did Travis Tritt. There were so many things he didn't know about his neighbor and he wanted to know everything. By the time the song ended he couldn't remember anything he'd heard. Every thought centered on something Stella had done in the past weeks.

That isn't part of the contract. Breakfast from six to seven, on the bar until eight if the clients arise a little later, no lunch, supper promptly at six, family style at the table, and BYOE, that's bring your own entertainment. This sounds like too many coincidences.

He remembered the way she brushed a wisp of unruly hair from her face when she poured tea for him. The way his hand tingled when he touched her fingers at the concert. And that defiant look on her face when she told him the way to get rid of a slug was to pour salt on it. And definitely the way she felt in his arms and the way she'd sighed when they shared those explosive kisses.

By the time he drove to Brannon Inn he'd begun to wonder if Mitch had rocks for brains. Stella was beautiful both inside and out. She was a fantastic lady even when she was angry. He thought about the look on her face when she and the mop were dancing around the bedroom to country music as he nosed his truck into the gravel driveway to the Brannon Inn.

Stella had opened the windows to air out the Inn in spite of the slight chill in the air earlier in the afternoon. To have a fifty degree day in December was an oddity and she wasn't wasting one bit of the sunshine. She had just lowered the last window when she saw headlights coming down the gravel lane to the Inn. Maggie and Lauren weren't in for the weekend, were they? She didn't have anyone booked and she'd planned on a quiet evening reading. One of those romance novels she'd checked out at the Sulphur library the day before. She had a choice. The newest by Nora Roberts, a Merline Lovelace or a Nancy Parra.

She prayed as she turned the lock on the

window. "Lord help me get Rance out of my heart and mind. Give me something in one of the books to think about other than his blue eyes."

The phone rang at the same time she heard the truck door slam. She picked up the phone and realized her heart was beating faster than usual. Mercy, she was surely getting out of shape when just putting down a window affected her like that. "Hello."

"Stella, hi honey. How's the Inn business?"

"Who is this?" She asked bluntly.

"Oh, I am truly hurt. Take you out, buy you an ice cream, look at the stars with you and even share a nice, warm kiss and you still don't recognize my voice? My heart is pained. Surely after seeing each other twice, you would remember my voice."

"Joel?" She said at the same time Rance knocked on the door. Talk about a horrid answer to a prayer. Rance in the room, making her blood boil with desire and Joel on the phone. Surely her prayer had gotten hung up on the rafters. God wouldn't send Joel to make her forget Rance. He didn't answer honest prayers with gag gifts.

He lowered his voice to barely above a sexy whisper. "Who else? At your service, ma'am. I thought we'd chase off to Dallas tomorrow afternoon, maybe have some supper and spend the night at a good motel. Then Sunday we'd take a leisurely drive back home. No little hints at pulling off the road. No kisses at the door of the Inn. Just a passionate weekend together."

"The answer is no and there's someone at my door." She breathed a sigh of pure relief which he took for disappointment.

"Then how about the next week?"

"I don't think so. I told you before it won't work. I don't like you and you really don't like me. Remember I'm too prudish and . . ."

"Okay, okay," he said, coldly. "But when you're sitting out there in twenty years with gray hair and wrinkles and no man will look at you, Stella, just remember you turned down the best offer you'll ever get."

"Temper, temper."

"Just facts, darlin'." He snapped. "Good-bye, Stella. Don't call me. I'll call you when I hear you've had a change of heart."

"Don't hold your breath. You look awful in that shade of blue. Good-bye, Joel."

Rance couldn't help hearing one side of the conversation through the screen door.

She turned abruptly and stared at him. "What are you doing here?"

"I'm on my way to town for some dinner.

Want to join me?" He gritted his teeth. Not at all the way he'd planned but dang it, she'd started the fight with her tone.

She shook her finger at him. "I told you at the hotel last week, this isn't going to work. We'll be friends or neighbors but I'm not dating you."

He put up his hands. "Hey, start all over. I'd like to go out for some dinner. Would you join me? It doesn't have to be a date. Just adult folks eating a meal together with a little conversation thrown in without a bunch of kids around."

"So you don't like kids? I might have known. Anyone so rich they're friends with Travis Tritt wouldn't want kids interrupting their dinner."

"I didn't say I didn't like kids." He protested. "And this is taking a way wrong turn. Let's catch our breath and start all over. Count to ten slowly. Both of us."

One. She's cute when she's angry. Two. I'll never be able to talk her into taking a step off the porch with me. Three. She's going to tell me to drop dead. Four. I guess I can make a peanut butter sandwich or heat up a can of soup since I sent the cook home and there's no food in the refrigerator. Five. I'm hungry. Six. I hope ten is far enough to cool off that hot temper of hers. Seven. Is she really interested in Joel and just playing hard to get? Eight. Maybe I better call for ten more cooling off seconds. Nine. She's going to pick up that plate of cookies and throw them in my face. Ten. Well here goes.

Stella set her mouth in a firm line and drew her eyebrows down into a furrow across her slender nose.

One. He's foolish to think I can cool down in ten seconds. Two. Maybe ten days. Three. More likely ten years. Four. He really doesn't look like Mitch and I'd like to kiss him again, but that's not even an option. Five. Why doesn't he just go away and stop making me want him? Six. I do like those blue eyes. Seven. I'd like to pick up this plate of cookies and throw them at him. Eight. I'm not ready to start over yet. Nine. I don't want him to affect me this way. Ten, well, here goes.

"Hello, Stella. Nice evening," he smiled brightly.

"Hello, Rance. Yes, it is," she said.

"You had supper yet?"

"No."

"That's good. We've said two whole sentences each and haven't blown up in anger yet. Since you haven't eaten, could I please take you to dinner? Name the place. Braum's for a hamburger. Sonic for a hot dog. Steak at wherever you want?"

"Why?"

"Because I'm hungry and you haven't eaten," he said casually.

"Sonic for a foot long cheese coney with onions, fries and a thick chocolate malt. If you've got a problem with people eating in your pickup then we'd better take mine."

He opened the door and stood aside. "No problem, my lady. Ready?"

She looked down at her jeans and sweat shirt with a picture of Bugs Bunny on the front. "You mean you'll actually go out in public, even just to Sonic with me looking like this?"

"Yes, ma'am, I surely will. You'd be beautiful in a gunny sack tied up in the middle with a piece of worn out rope," he drawled in pure Texas fashion. "Got a jacket? And don't forget your key. We don't want to get locked out and spend the night huddled up on the porch swing."

"Why?"

"Because it's getting cold and you might need your jacket," he said.

"No, why wouldn't you want to have to spend the night huddled up with me on a porch swing?"

"Hey, you're the one who called the shots, Stella. You said there was no future so you didn't want a present. I'm just asking for company while I have supper."

"Fair enough." But deep down she wished she could change her mind. Being his girlfriend might not be such a bad idea.

Not on your life, lady. I want the whole ball of wax this time. Not a wannabe actor or a spawn of the devil like Joel. Just a good man to make my heart do double time and . . . oh forget it. I called the shots. Now I'll have to live with them.

She grabbed a gray zippered sweat shirt from the back of a chair, picked up keys from the sideboard and shook them at him. She wasn't sure if she'd just been roped into a date or if he'd offered out of gratitude that she hadn't blown her stack at the end of the ten second intermission from the argument. If it was the former then he'd wish he hadn't offered by the time she asked for extra onions on her hot dog. Maybe that's where she went wrong when she went out with Joel. She should have ordered a hamburger instead of ice cream and piled on the onions, then when he kissed her he would have fainted in a fog of bad breath.

Rance opened the door to his truck for her and then whistled all the way around to the driver's side. That hadn't been so hard and he really did like Sonic hot dogs, but seldom ate them. Usually when he asked a lady out they expected a nice restaurant with real tablecloths and napkins. In his wildest dreams, he couldn't visualize his ex-wife eating a greasy hot dog at Sonic. Not even if it was part of a modeling contract and they offered her megabucks.

He attempted a bit of conversation as he drove. "Did you have a good time the rest of the weekend in Dallas? I thought I might see you in the restaurant the next morning at breakfast."

"Yes, I did have a good time. We ate late and barely made check out time," she said. If she had to answer twenty one questions just to get a foot long hot dog, it would be one tedious meal.

"Did you run into that fellow from the concert again?"

"No." She said honestly and then wished she lied and said they'd spent the whole weekend together.

"That's nice." He started whistling "Rose Colored Glasses".

That same song had been on her mind that day as she cleaned the rooms and got ready for the next bunch of boarders due Sunday night. It was as if he'd invaded her mind, stealing her thoughts, her songs and her desires; upsetting her entire world.

He turned to her once they were parked

at the Sonic. "Name your poison. I'll push the button so you have to think fast . . ."

A tinny voice came over the speaker outside the car. "Sonic, may I help you?"

Stella leaned past Rance and delivered her own order. "A foot long coney with extra onions, cheese and chili, tator tots and an extra thick chocolate malt." She touched his thigh for support and a jolt flowed all the way up her arm to her neck. She pulled her hand away and resisted the urge to look at the palm to see if it was burned.

"Your turn," she mumbled.

"Double that order. And add a cup of coffee."

"We're going to fog the windows with onion breath." She watched a group of high school kids gather around a low slung sports car.

"Quarter for your thoughts," Rance said.

She turned her big blue eyes around to really look at him, sitting so close she could reach out and touch his five o'clock shadow. "It's a penny."

"Not in today's world. A penny's worth of thought wouldn't buy even a dumb blond joke. No offense meant about your hair color. So with inflation I'm offering a whole quarter for whatever it was that made you look so wistfully across the grass and toward that little red car. You like sport's cars or just Mustangs in particular?" Rance asked.

"Neither. I was thinking about those kids. Oh, to be that young and naive. To have all that confidence and be ready to set the world on fire. The most important thing in their life is whether to paint their fingernails blue or purple or which earrings to wear."

"Or whether or not their father is really going to let him drive his brand new sports car to the Sonic to impress all the girls with purple fingernails," Rance finished for her.

"Amen."

"So tell me Stella, would you really go back and do it all over again?"

She shook her head. "Not for a guaranteed ride to the pearly gates. Once through that was enough. It's just that they are so cocky and sure. I'd like to have that again. To know without even a little shadow of doubt; to make a decision without thinking about how it's going to affect the whole rest of my life."

"It is a magical age, isn't? Did you hang around here when you were growing up?"

"Yes, I did. At least some of the time. Sulphur's not very big so every body knows everyone else. What about you? Bet you went to a big school in Waco," she asked.

"Actually I grew up in Grapevine. Went to

the Grapevine High School. Home of the Grapevine Mustangs. Four-A school. Probably only a little bigger than Sulphur. But close enough to Dallas and big enough that we really didn't know everyone. Just almost. Here comes supper. We may have to go to Wal-Mart for mouth wash by the time we finish all those onions," he laughed.

"Oh, they serve peppermints, but it would take a ton to fight what we're about to do." She reached for the foot long hot dog he handed her and bit into the end of it. "Mmmm. This is wonderful."

He followed her lead, and bit into the aromatic chili dog. "It looks like it is."

"And be danged to fat grams and calories." She said between bites. "Who cares about all that when there's good food in front of a body?"

"Yes, yes, yes," he said. He couldn't remember the last time he'd eaten inside his truck like a teenager at a Sonic, much less taken a lady there with him, or when food had tasted so good. "What happened after you finished eating here when you were a kid?"

She popped a hot tator tot in her mouth. "Oh, we'd go to the park and put our toes in the water, but honey, not even a whole band of angels could talk me into dipping my bare feet in Little Niagara in the winter. It'll freeze the horns off Lucifer himself on July 4, so we won't be wading or skinny dipping at this time of year."

"Chicken?" He teased.

"Nope, just sensible. We'll go through the park and I'll even let you dip your hand in the water and then you'll believe me," she said. She could have kicked herself for suggesting such a thing. A non-date didn't include a moonlight visit to the park with someone like Rance.

"Sounds good. We might breathe on the water and make it a lot warmer," he said.

They finished their hot dogs and tator tots and were sipping malts as they drove back through Sulphur and turned south into the park. She showed him which turns to make and in a few minutes they were sitting in the only vehicle in a parking lot beside a bubbling stream rushing down over a small waterfall. Not even by stretching the imagination and maybe closing one eye could it actually look like a very, very small specimen of Niagara Falls. She was out of the truck before he could open the door and headed for the water.

She sat down at the edge of the water, and pulled her jacket close around her. "I love the smell of water and night air at the same time." She dipped her fingers in the water and whistled backwards through her teeth.

He sat down beside her, keeping a foot between them. He wanted to draw her close even just for a hug but even with two peppermints he could exhale on a drunk and put him to sleep for a week. He stuck his hand into the water and instantly believed her story about the cold. "Wow, it is cold. Did you really skinny dip in this place?"

"Couple of times," she said. "But it was in July or August, not winter time. And it was after a couple of beers."

"Can we come back tomorrow? How about some hiking? We'll pick up breakfast at Braum's and bring it with us in a paper bag. We're supposed to have another warm day tomorrow and then there's a norther blowing down from Kansas."

"Okay." She agreed then could have thrown herself into the cold water for such a rash decision, but the damage was already done, and besides if she was honest with herself, she might enjoy a day out.

"We'll bring some cookies and I'll pack us a sandwich." She planned aloud. "And whoever tuckers out first has to buy supper tomorrow night at wherever I say." She knew she was playing with fire and yet had absolutely no power over her words.

He wiped his freezing hand on the leg of his jeans and stuck it out. "Deal."

She did the same. "Deal."

Neither was prepared for the heat flowing from one body to the other in spite of the cool night air or their cold hands.

CHAPTER SIX

The alarm clock started a mechanical beep at five o'clock and Rance groaned, swatted at the snooze button with his right hand and pulled the pillow over his head with his left one. Then he remembered what had been planned for that day and threw the pillow in the floor, sat straight up in bed and tossed the covers off to the side. He jerked on his sweatshirt and jeans, pulled on a pair of socks and his athletic shoes and combed his black hair back with his fingers. He'd shaven the night before and his face was only slightly rough but he could take care of that in the evening before they went to dinner. Which he intended to pay for, even if she did out hike, out walk, and out do him all day long in the park.

"Well, good morning. Thought you might have reneged and decided to sleep all day." She teased when he arrived at the Inn.

Her heart skipped a beat when she looked

up from the swing. Well, it could just carry on like that if it wanted. At the end of a day of hiking and talking, she was sure she'd have him completely washed from her mind and life. Give her a whole day with him and she'd find at least a million things she hated, and that would be that. God had heard her prayer after all.

Rance could scarcely believe how beautiful she was in the cool morning air. The sun barely rising behind the house threw just enough light to let him see all her features, including a full sensuous mouth and the biggest bluest eyes in the whole state of Oklahoma.

He propped a hip up on the porch railing. "Did you even go to bed? I figured I'd find you still asleep."

"Get up every morning at five o'clock. Remember I have breakfast to fix by six. Already got the cookies in the bag and I know a special place on Travertine Island where we can eat. You ready?"

"At your mercy, Miss Stella. I thought we were going to the park. What's this Travertine Island?"

"Part of the park. Good thing you got a jacket with you. Weatherman said there's a twenty percent chance of rain and it feels like he might be right for a change. At least

114

it's not supposed to freeze. That usually doesn't happen until the the first of January." She stood up and stretched her long arms above her head.

He gasped at the feelings it evoked. The sheer catlike motion mesmerized him in a way no other woman ever had. Not even Julie and she was a professional model. But when Julie moved it was with the grace of years and years of classes, tutoring and experience. When Stella stretched or cocked her head that certain way, it was as natural and unaffected as his two cats, stretching in the morning sun.

"Give me a couple of minutes to get our backpacks," she said.

He waited on the porch. Talk about a different kind of woman. Most of the women he'd known, including his ex-wife, would have had to check their makeup one more time, and stood in front of the floor length mirror worrying one hair to death trying to keep it behind her ear. Stella didn't have a smidgen of makeup on; no lipstick, which suited Rance just fine. He hated to kiss lipstick. Especially if it had just been applied. He felt like he was sinking his lips into a bowl of greased Jell-O.

She returned and handed him a small black backpack. "Take this. It's your breakfast and dinner, a bottle of real water because you probably won't like the Sulphur water. It tastes like it's been laced with rotten eggs. And I've also put in a couple of snacks in case you need a little sustenance along the way."

"And where's your dinner and breakfast? Am I carrying enough in this little bitty pack to feed us both?" He raised a dark eyebrow.

"I carry my own." She held up proof in a bright, hot pink backpack. "You, kind sir, will have enough to do this day just keeping up with me. You don't need the added burden of my daily needs."

"Then let us be off to the wilds." He led the way to his truck.

The sun was a bright orange ball peeking through the long limbs on the bare trees by the time they'd scouted most of the small island in the middle of the park. She sat down on a fallen tree log and declared it was time for breakfast.

"You will find a brown paper sack marked with a big B for breakfast," she said.

He pulled out the right bag the first time. "Breakfast! Is that really bacon I smell? I thought we were having cookies."

She nodded. "Yes, it's bacon. Stuffed inside two big biscuits. Coffee in the small thermos, and then six of those cookies. That should keep you until lunch. So what do you think of this tiny, little island? We're the only ones on it right now."

Her honest smile caused his heart to do one of those crazy flip-flops that thirty year old men weren't supposed to experience anymore. That was for sixteen year old boys. Mature men didn't react like that and he promised he'd give his heart a good lecture later on that night.

"It's not The Bahamas but I expect we could live for half a day here with the help of a couple of these." He bit into the cold biscuit. The bacon was done to perfection, crispy and drained well. "You are a good cook, Stella. Would you consider leaving the Inn and jumping the fence to live with me and be my cook?"

She shook her head. "Nope, I'm not up for hire. Living or cooking."

"Let me know if you ever are," he said. "Hey, look at that squirrel. I think he smells the bacon."

"Probably. Or the cookies. They're spoiled to handouts. Even though it's not a good thing. They need to forage for themselves on what nature provides." She whispered while she broke a peanut butter cookie in half and tossed it closer to the squirrel.

"Yep," he said, thinking that he should be

taking the advice himself. Foraging for life amongst what fate had put before him. Who would have ever thought that he'd find someone like Stella when he bought the old Morgan ranch? And how did he convince her that he was seriously interested in more than a few kisses?

"Where to next?" Rance finished the last drop of coffee.

"You are in for a hike. We're going to Bromide Hill and back."

"Bromide Hill? Sounds like a place teenagers go to park after they've been to the movies." He glanced up and caught her looking at him. He could swim forever in the cool blue of her eyes.

She nodded, a prickle starting at the base of her neck and crawling upward like a tickle all the way through her hair to her forehead. "It is but it's a good steep hike, too. I imagine that if teenagers hiked up there rather than drove, it would cool their hormones a lot."

They marched side by side, through pathways and tip-toeing across creeks on mossy covered rocks, until they reached the top of the hill. She sat down Indian style in a bed of crispy, crinkly scrub oak leaves and opened her backpack.

"Time to eat again. Sustenance to hold us

until we get back to the Island." She rested her eyes on the naked trees waiting for spring to come and touch them with green buds. She loved spring, loved the rebirth of the trees, the baby kittens who showed up somewhere in the woodpile next to the smokehouse every year about that time, and even that wonderful feeling inside her heart telling her another dead season had passed. But she loved winter, too, with the naked trees and brisk winds.

"Mmmmm." He made grateful noises when he opened a chicken salad sandwich and a bottle of pure well water from the Inn. The Sulphur water made his nose itch just smelling it, and when he actually put it in his mouth just to prove to her he was big and man enough to do so, he thought he'd knock a toenail off from shivering.

Stella told him that in the old days people came from miles and miles around to draw the water into containers to take home since it was supposed to cure everything from ingrown toenails to baldness. And they also arrived from everywhere to bathe in the water, thinking it could wipe out all kinds of illnesses.

He had said he'd take his chances with penicillin pills and she laughed, that low, husky, sexy way that sent his senses reeling.

"Just enough calories to get us back home, and then it looks like supper might be a draw since I haven't tuckered you plumb out yet," she said.

He nodded and finished his sandwich, took a big red apple out of the sack and bit into it. "It's peaceful up here. Are you really going to get married again some day?"

She jerked her head around to look at him. Now why did he have to ask a stupid question like that and spoil everything? She started to ignore him but answered before she thought. "Are you? Have you not found someone you trust with your babies?"

"Nope." He grinned.

She wanted to shoot him. Just who took care of those babies? He probably had a nanny who cared for them, who they ran to when they had boo-boos on their knees, who saw them take their first step and held them while they cried when they cut their teeth. When Stella had children she wouldn't leave them with another woman. She'd be condemned to a barbed wire fence on the back forty acres of hell before she ever left her children.

"What's so funny?" She snapped.

He continued to grin. "My babies."

She glared at him wordlessly, then turned her back and furiously ate an apple. How dare he act like something as precious as a child could be a laughing matter. This day was a mistake after all. Rance Harper was a mistake.

"My babies are Melanie and Grace," he finally said.

Something squeezed her heart so bad her chest ached: two daughters.

"They're both alley cats. I rescued them from the horse stables when their mother died. One is black and white and one is orange. I had to feed them with one of those little tiny bottles and special milk I got from our vet. Until their eyes opened I even had to get up in the middle of the night. By the time they could lap out of a saucer, I thought I'd taken on the care of real babies. They sleep with me and I spoil them as rotten as if they were real kids. Did you really think I had children?"

"Yes, I did." She admitted, the heaviness rising from her chest and leaving a song in its place.

"So are you going to answer me about getting married again now that we have my paternity straightened out?"

"When you answer me. But then, I heard why you won't remarry when you were at the inn with that hiker family. Something like once bit, twice shy. And no tall blondes.

So I assume your ex-wife was a tall blond. Self-proclaimed bachelor who intends to climb the Pearly Gates without a woman dragging along on his coat tails. Did I remember it all right?"

Rance held up his hands in defence. "Yes, you remembered it just fine. Bill was protecting me from that little dark haired vampire. Okay, truth is, I haven't remarried because I'm scared to death of commitment like I told you before. Your turn."

"Because no man can offer what I want, like I told you before," she said.

"And that's one of those lifetime things?"

"Yep. The very thing that scares the devil out of you and all the male species. That sends ya'll flying back to your trucks so fast you'd think you had sprouted wings. All I have to do is mention that phrase and you'll leave nothing in your wake but a fear of ever returning."

"Whew. You do speak your mind. You're not interested in money and power?"

"Nope. That's the last thing I want." She stared out over the country side.

From the angle he sat he could see her blue eyes floating in tears, but she was stubborn enough not to let even one spill over the dam. Part of him knew he should be the one to change the subject. To say, 'Hey, let's talk about something lighter. Like where are we going for supper?' But another part wanted to know the whole answer so he waited.

"So if you can't start out a relationship with a lifetime thing then you don't even want to begin it?" He asked again.

"I want it all, Rance. Every smidgen bit of it. I want a commitment and every little tiny thing that goes with it. I want someone I can trust. Someone I can believe. Someone who won't walk into our home five years after we're married and say 'I want a divorce because you are a hindrance to my career.' I want someone who comes home every night and I don't even have to ask if I'm the best thing that happened to him that day. I want to see it in his eyes when he takes his boots off at the door. I want to wake up every morning with something inside me that knows this is real and permanent. I want a baby nine months after I get married and at least three more after that. One every year until there's four of them in the house. I want it all! Do you understand? No, you couldn't possibly understand. Because you're a man and to understand you'd have to feel with your heart and open up your soul. In essence what I want, Rance, is really that lifetime thing. Something to last through all eternity, and I haven't found a man yet who's got a lifetime thing to offer."

He whistled through his teeth. "Whew! Guess I really asked for that, didn't I?"

"You laid down and begged for it," she said shortly. "I guess I really crawled up on my soap box and let you have it, didn't I?"

"Stepped right up and spoke your mind. I'll have to ponder over what you said a few days."

"You do that Rance," she told him. "And if there's an old ugly cowboy that you know who'll fit that kind of bill, kick him over the fence and I might take a shine to him."

Stella dressed in the electric blue silk pants suit she bought at Sak's in Dallas, and brushed her hair until it was shiny. She slapped a little bit of makeup on her face and noticed that she'd gotten a bit sunburned that day. At least it waited to rain until they gotten back to the Inn. A hard, driving rain complete with thunder and lightning hit not fifteen minutes after she was safe inside. Even yet, a fine drizzle still fell outside so she picked up an umbrella standing in an old pickling crock beside her bedroom door before she started downstairs.

She'd just opened her bedroom door

when the telephone rang. Holding the umbrella in one hand, she grabbed the phone and answered, "Hello, Brannon Inn."

"Well, well, who squatted in your oatmeal this morning?" Her mother laughed. "And what's this I hear about you wandering all over the park with some dark haired stranger? Is your mother the last to know when you've found a feller after all this time? And I just heard talk in town that Joel was panting around your back door."

"Mercy!" Stella exclaimed. "So many questions. So little time. I'm about to go to dinner with that dark haired stranger. His name is Rance Harper and he's not my feller. He was a boarder and now he is my neighbor. He bought the old Morgan ranch next door. And Joel can pant until his tongue dries out. I'm not interested in him or anything he's got."

"Well, have a good time. I'll be over tomorrow afternoon for a full report, so don't forget any details. And I'll call Maggie to bring the gun. I think the words which fell from your lips when you came home was, 'If I ever look at another good-looking, dark haired man with brown eyes, just shoot me between the eyes, roll me up in a quilt and throw me in a bar ditch.' And we wouldn't want to disregard your wishes," her mother said.

"You leave Maggie out of this," Stella scolded. "Please tell me she and Lauren didn't beat a path down here just to give me a lecture?"

"Maggie and Lauren are already on the way. But I haven't called your brother, yet, but if you're in a fighting mood that means you must like this feller. I might ought to call a family pow-wow before we shoot you. What time tomorrow would be good for the family gathering?"

"Not until supper time." She intoned with a heavy sigh.

"I'll bring your favorite chicken salad. The one with cool whip and I'll even bake a loaf of fresh rye bread. We'll pick up ice cream at Braums for dessert. You make the coffee. Have a nice evening, my daughter. Where is this knight in shining armor from?"

"Grapevine, Texas, and no more questions. Good-bye, Mother." She hung up the phone.

She stole glances at Rance while he drove through Sulphur and west to Davis. His jeans were starched to perfection, and there was a tuft of dark hair peeking out the top of his pale gray western shirt. She could practically see herself in the toes of his boots and she had the insane desire to scoot right across the wide bench seat and snuggle up close to him. But after that tirade on Bromide Hill, he'd probably wreck the truck trying to crawl out the door to get away from her. As a matter of fact, as quiet as he'd been she would probably never hear from him again after tonight.

"Turn right at the red light." She told him in the middle of downtown Davis and he snapped his head around to look at her. "It's that little restaurant on your right in the stone building."

"Right here?" he asked. "I thought we were going to some fancy steak house."

She pointed to the only lit up building on that side of the street, the one just past the car wash. "We're going right there. And when you've tasted their food, you won't be disappointed. Trust me?"

"Yes, ma'am, your wish is my pure Texas desire." He nosed his truck into a parking place between an old beat up Ford Maverick and a big white Caddy.

"Hi, Stella, where you been girl? Haven't seen you in months. Must be keepin' you busy at the Inn." A waitress called from behind the long counter of The Main Street Restaurant.

Rance tried to take in the place with a

127

quick glance around the surroundings, but it was impossible. Every square inch of wall space was covered with old memorabilia. Farm equipment, old baking tins, movie posters, even a big, faded picture of the Declaration of Independence, and posters of movie stars. Stella herded him into a booth, tossing her purse in one side and sliding in beside it. The waitress brought menus and water in tall, red plastic glasses. One of those old paper napkin dispensers, salt and pepper shakers and a bottle of hot sauce were to his right. He hadn't seen a place like this in years.

"So what looks good?" She peeped over the top of her menu to find her mother and sister walking in the front door. Her mother frowned and nudged Maggie. They sat down at a booth in the front of the restaurant.

"What do you suggest?" He asked.

"Oh, I like their T-bones, salad with honey mustard dressing, maybe some red beans and fried okra on the side and a nice big baked potato with sour cream and butter. Then we can ask if there's any coconut cream pie left. It goes fast."

"If that's what you like, then I'll have the same thing. Make my steak rare."

The waitress appeared. "Regular, right?

And double?"

Stella nodded. "That's right."

The waitress disappeared into the kitchen and Stella sipped at the water. "My mother and sister just walked in the door and are sitting in a front booth. I haven't seen my sister in two months because she lives in Kansas. Would you mind?"

He slid out of the booth and waited for her. "Let's go talk to them."

"You don't have to go."

"But I want to." He slipped his arm around her waist and she shivered. Her mother would never, ever hush about Rance now.

She leaned down and hugged her sister. "Hi! I didn't know you'd be here this early. Momma said you were on the way, but I thought it might be late."

"Oh, no. Lauren has a date with some pimply faced kid and heaven help us if we were a minute late," Maggie said.

"This is Rance Harper." Stella introduced him and immediately saw her mother's disapproval and a look from her sister. There would definitely be a lecture tomorrow night. "Rance, this is my mother, Lucy Brannon and my sister, Maggie."

Rance shook hands with them both. "I'm pleased to make your acquaintance."

Lucy smiled tightly and Maggie mumbled the right words.

Yes, sir, it would be the deluxe lecture. She deliberately switched places with him when they returned to their booth. Rance could deal with the frown on her mother's face. She wasn't about to spoil her steak with her mother's discouraging leers.

The waitress brought their dinner and stopped long enough to talk to Stella a few minutes then she was off to visit with another customer. They'd no more than cut the first bite of steak when Stella felt a warm hand on her shoulder and revulsion when she looked up to see Joel sliding into the booth beside her. He picked up a cherry tomato from the edge of her salad and popped it into his mouth.

He nodded toward Rance. "So hi, honey. Who's this? A cousin?"

"This is Rance Harper, and no, he is not my cousin. He's the man you met at the Inn a few weeks ago. We are having dinner and we don't want a third wheel," Stella said bluntly.

"My, my testy, ain't we, sweetheart. I didn't recognize Lance. Well, old Joel will just wait his turn. Just don't let Lance get too close to my merchandise." He kissed her on the cheek and went back to the front of the restaurant to sit with her mother and sister.

"Didn't know I'd moved in on someone else's merchandise," Rance said.

"I'm not. We're not. It's a figment of his overactive imagination. I've told him I'm not interested. He's just got a big ego and can't bear to have it deflated."

"Good enough. This is a great place, Stella. Do you know everyone in the whole county?"

"Pretty close."

"Anyone ever tell you that if you cut your hair a little you'd look somewhat like her?" He pointed to a picture of Marilyn Monroe sitting on a bar stool at the Hollywood Diner.

"Then you need glasses," she said with a giggle. "But I'll play along. Did anyone ever tell you that you look like Elvis, who's right beside her?"

"Ah, shucks. I just knew you'd say I looked like James Dean, not Elvis."

"With all that black hair and those eyes? James Dean had lighter hair."

"But don't you think my nose is like his?" Rance stopped eating and tilted his head to the side so she could see his profile.

"About like my legs are like Marilyn Monroe's," she said.

"Well, show them to me and we'll compare," he teased.

"In your dreams, cowboy."

They drove to the top of Bromide Hill on the way back to the Inn but she still couldn't drag up the nerve to slide across the seat and sit close to him. She berated herself for being prudish and even childish. Grown up women in today's world didn't act like this, but she still didn't make a move. Merciful heavens, she didn't dare. If she touched him, she'd roll over on her back and it would all be over but the afterglow.

"Doesn't take nearly so long to drive here as to walk." He commented as they drove back toward the main road.

"No." She watched a star fall from the heavens. She had a wish coming. What would she wish for? One of those ugly cowboys who had a lifetime thing hiding down in his soul?

"Did you see that star?"

She cocked her head to one side and looked even more like Marilyn Monroe in the pale moonlight. "Yes, I did, and I saw it before you so it's my wish."

"What are you going to wish for?" He asked.

"What do you think I'd wish for?"

"No fair answering a question with a question."

"I shall wish for one of those ugly cowboys to ride to Sulphur, Oklahoma on a big white horse and bring me a lifetime thing," she said.

He shook his head. "Does he have to be ugly?"

"Probably. Handsome cowboys don't want lifetime things," she said.

When Rance nosed his truck into the yard at Brannon Inn someone stood up from the porch swing. Stella thought at first it was Lauren and was worried that maybe she'd had a bad experience with her date. Then she realized the girl was dark haired and entirely too short to be her niece. She felt Rance stiffened and she squinted but still didn't recognize the lady.

"Damn!" Rance swore under his breath. "You said the Inn was vacant for the whole weekend."

"It is."

"Then what is she doing here?" He asked.

"Who is she?" Stella asked.

Rance was still mumbling when he got out of the truck and walked around to open the door for her.

The girl stepped off the porch. "Hi. Got a

room for the night for a weary hiker?"

"Jewel?" Stella suddenly remembered.

"Miss Branscum, how are you? And *hellllllo,* Rance. I didn't know you were here for the weekend. Didn't see any lights but figured you'd be home after a while. Miss Branscum, I'd like a room for the night."

"We're booked solid," Rance said. "No vacancy at the Inn tonight."

"Oh?" Jewel raised an eyebrow. "*We* are booked solid. Who is *we?* I don't see any cars."

"Folks are out until late," Stella lied. "Besides this isn't a motel or a hotel. People stay here by reservation only."

"Imagine that. Well, guess I better get on down the road toward Sulphur. I'll be at the motel there. Want to come along Rance? We could do an instant replay of our last time." She edged over to him and looped her arm through his.

He took her arm out of his and dropped it. "No thank you."

"Well, then don't blame me if you can't get to sleep just thinking about what you turned down. And good night to you, Miss Branscum. Bet you sleep good tonight. Old folks usually don't stay out this late. My mother says if she's not in bed by ten she's horrible the next day. Be seeing you, Rance.

I'll call next week and see if you're busy." She waved and disappeared around the corner of the Inn toward her black Bronco.

Stella opened the door and stomped inside. Then as suddenly as the anger filled her soul, it disappeared and she felt like she was sitting on top of the world. So little Jewel had wanted her to believe she had been out with Rance? She bet Brannon Inn that she was lying by the look of exasperation and even desperation on his face. Stella couldn't even be mad at her. After all what young girl wouldn't like all that money and power?

Rance grimaced. "Guess I owe you an apology. I'm sorry. She called me last week and wanted me to take her to dinner. I declined. Must have upset her."

"You might be passing over a wonderful opportunity."

"I don't think so."

She leaned forward and kissed him on the cheek and kept her hands clasped behind her back. If she ever got close enough to hug him or if he kissed her on the mouth again, she feared she'd drag him up the stairs. "Well, thank you for a lovely day. And for a wonderful evening. We've both eaten our toad frogs tonight, so let's go to bed and get some sleep."

135

He raised both eyebrows. "Together?"

"No, sir. You wouldn't want to sleep with an ancient old girl who might snore," she threw over her shoulder as she unlocked the front door. "Us motherly figures have to get our rest you know."

"What was that about toad frogs? Why did we eat toad frogs?"

"Granny said to get up every morning and eat a toad frog and the rest of the day would go wonderfully well. Well, we ate ours. Mine's name is Joel and yours is Jewel. Maybe we should introduce them to each other."

He tipped an imaginary hat. "Sounds good to me. Good night, Miss Branscum."

She curtsied in the doorway. "Good night to you, Lance."

CHAPTER SEVEN

Stella bundled up in a quilt her grand-mother had made years before and kept a steady rhythm with her foot on the porch swing. She'd really run Rance off for sure. He'd never even hinted that he wanted more than a passing fancy so it was no surprise that he wasn't interested in her soap box soliloquy about a future that stretched on for eternity.

She heard the truck before it turned down her lane. That would be her sister, Maggie, and Lauren, coming to pave the way for the steam roller called Lucy Brannon who'd be out for blood today. She'd told them to wait until supper but that wasn't Lucy's style. She plowed right into everyone's business and said exactly what she thought.

When she looked up it was Rance getting out of the truck, shaking the legs of his dress slacks down over his boot and feathering back his dark hair with his fingers. Rance, all dressed up, took her breath away.

"Hey, did you lock yourself out and have to sit on the porch all night?" He asked.

"No, I'm here because I want to be, not because I have to be."

"Thought you might be in church this morning. I'm on my way home."

"Should have been but I overslept. Us old women do that sometimes."

"You go to the Baptist church in Sulphur?"

"Yes, I do. Did you see Dee there?"

"Saw a red haired woman named Roxie who said to tell you she missed you and to say hello, and her granddaughter . . . yes, that was Dee, and her husband, Jack. Met a lot more folks but those are the ones I remember. Guess it's because they said to say hello to you. So here I am saying it."

"Thank you."

"Who are Dee and Roxie?"

She moved to the far end of the swing. "Have a seat and I'll tell you."

"Come to lunch with me and tell me there."

"No thanks. I'll be your friend and tell you the county secrets but I'm not going to lunch with you."

He sat down and waited.

Stella gave him time to get comfortable

and then started the history lesson. "Roxie married young and moved out here during the oil boom. Her husband died and she bought a big old house down the road, put in a bed and breakfast and called it Roxie's B&B. Stood for bed and breakfast, but those of us who know her said it stood for belly-achin's and blessin's. She has a daily ritual and has a lemonade on the porch every day when the sun sets. She had a young daughter named Mimosa who's about my mother's age. She raised her in the bed and breakfast and eventually Mimosa ran away with a truck driver. When she gave birth to Tallulalah . . . we call her Tally . . . she brought her home for Roxie to raise. A few years later she had Dee . . . real name is Delylah . . . and did the same. Roxie said if she was raising the girls they had to be named Hooper so that's why they have the same name as she does. Anyway, last year Dee's husband, one of those damn Yankees, came home one day and kicked her out. His old love had returned and he wanted to be married to her so his mega-rich parents bought him an annulment. Dee came home and fell in love with the boy next door who is Jack. But before all that Tally eloped with a country music wannabe and moved to Nashville. She's got the face and body to be

139

one of those high powered singers but her voice is thin. Anyway, she had a baby girl and brought it home to Roxie. Little girl named Bodine. When she found out she couldn't sing, she came home and she played around with one thing and another until she got into trouble for hot checks. Spent a year in county lock up for it and when she got out Roxie said she had to go to college. So she met a professor and they got married. Now they live in Tishomingo and Bodine loves it. Jack and Dee are expecting their first baby. And Mimosa is off with another truck driver. This one seems to be lasting longer than the rest. Roxie retired just before Granny Brannon died."

"That's not a story. That's a mini-series for television. Where'd they ever come up with names like that? Roxie looks like a Roxie all right, like the madam of a brothel. But Dee is just as sweet and pregnant as she can be. But Tallulah and Bodine. Not to mention Mimosa. Good Lord!"

"Be careful. Dee would have your sorry hide tacked to the smoke house door if you called Roxie a madam. She took out a little girl in grade school for the same thing and she didn't even know what a madam was back in those days. As for the rest of the names, I have no idea. Roxie and Granny Etta and my Granny Brannon were the self-crowned queens of the three original old bed and breakfast joints around here. They were competitive but best friends. Met about once a week for coffee and sent us girls out to play. I stayed with Granny Brannon most weekends. Dee lived with Roxie. And the third one, Roseanna Cahill, Etta's granddaughter, lived on the same property with her granny so she was over at the lodge as much as she was in her own house. Granny Etta is talking about closing down the Cahill Lodge after this winter, so that will be the end of an era."

"Thank you for sharing all that. Don't know that I'll keep it all straight but when Roxie winks at me in church again, I'll know some of the background. Does she always dress that flamboyant?"

"Roxie, flamboyant? She's just Roxie. She's a true southern lady. Hats and gloves on Sunday. Keep your Caddy spotless. One drink a day. And as trashy as Dolly Parton," she ended with a giggle.

Rance joined in the laughter. "I believe it. Sure you don't want to do lunch?"

"Positive. I'm going to sit here a while longer then read a book all day."

"Then enjoy it," Rance waved goodbye.

A dark Blazer turned down the lane as Rance pulled away. She'd been right. Rance was not a lifetime thing, not one to ever jump over the hurdle of the 'C' word with her, but he might be a wonderful friend and neighbor.

She waved at her niece, Lauren. She fought back a crazy tear forming somewhere in the pit of her aching heart. Aching for what couldn't be. Was she plumb goofy for ever thinking it could be possible? "Hey, girl. Come in and let's have some cookies. Did you eat lunch after church?"

Lauren nodded. "Ricky and I went to the Sonic but he had to go to work at one so I told Momma I was coming over here. Was that the devil with the horns and a pitchfork? He didn't look like he was out to tear you up and spit your heart out in pieces."

Stella patted the other side of the swing in invitation. "Guess they weren't impressed. So how was the date with Ricky? And church this morning and then lunch? Sounds pretty serious to me."

"Could be in ten years," Lauren said seriously. "I like him a lot, but I've got a couple more years of high school then a long, long haul in med school. And Ricky has to finish this year in high school then he's going to be a vet."

"Smart girl."

"Smart? It looks like forever on this end and sometimes it's not so easy to be smart, not when you like someone as much as I like him."

"Need to talk girl stuff?"

"Nope, just need to keep reminding myself to keep all these raging teenage hormones in check. That's what Granny and mother say. That I'm the age when my hormones are raging and I need to be careful. It's not easy though, is it Aunt Stella?"

"Don't matter what age you are, it's never easy to tell yourself no when it wants something."

Lauren stood up. "What's his name? They just called him a dark haired devil."

"His name is Rance Harper and he's really a nice man. He's just not interested in the same thing I am so it's not going anywhere. I could really like him, but it's not written in the stars. We're on different planes and times," Stella said.

"Ricky is nice, too. You never know, Aunt Stella, what tomorrow holds. If you like him, it could work. Let's do a *Lethal Weapon* marathon this afternoon. Cookies, popcorn and tea and good old Mel. By the time Momma and Granny get here, we'll be ready to . . ."

". . . fight to the last draw," Stella finished for her. "You watch the first one while I clean up a room and get ready for people coming in late tonight. I'll join you for the rest or as much as we have time for before the cavalry arrives."

"You mean he didn't sleep upstairs with you?" Lauren teased. "I figured he was already using his wicked ways to seduce you."

Stella shook her finger at Lauren. "No, he did not."

Once inside, Stella arranged cookies on a plate, poured the boiling water over the tea and took both to the coffee table. "It won't take me long. Just have to put the finishing touches on the other rooms and clean one."

She opened the door to a faint whisper of the previous boarder's shaving lotion. It wasn't like the spicy scent Mitch wore or even that overpowering odor that preceded Joel into the room. It was a warm, woodsy smell: what Rance wore. She inhaled deeply and remembered his touch at the restaurant when he put his arm around her in the restaurant.

Maybe he would call later.

Probably not.

His good-bye sounded pretty final.

She pulled the covers from the bed, threw

them in a pile on the floor and went to the hall linen closet for fresh ones. When she returned she noticed one of the pillows on the recliner. She picked it up, held it under her chin to strip the case off and got a nose full of the lingering cologne which brought a clearer vision of him.

It might not be easy, like Lauren said, but she was a strong woman. If nothing else, Mitch had made her strong that fatal evening he waltzed into the living room and declared that she needed to pack and get out. When the first rays of dawn filtered through the windows the next day, she had a choice. Get on with life. Or go upstairs and use one of Mitch's pistols. Really quit breathing. She chose living.

She muttered as she jerked the clean sheets on the bed. "Why does everything remind me of Rance? Why am I attracted to men with dark hair and who act like they're God's gift to the whole female race?"

It has nothing to do with what color his hair is or his eyes. Shut your eyes, Stella Sue Brannon. Don't even think about his hair or the fact he resembles Mitch ever so slightly. Think about him . . . the person. Think about the way he makes you feel.

She shut her eyes then snapped them open and attempted to push Rance from her mind as she finished cleaning the room. When she finished she found Lauren asleep on the couch; not snoring, but curled up in a ball with a pillow under her head and hugging another one like a long, lost brother. Lauren was her favorite. She was Maggie's only child. Her brother, Martin, had two boys, Jim and Bob, and she loved them. Crystal, her oldest sister, had a daughter, Katy, who was only five years younger than Stella. They all lived in Virginia so Stella didn't see them often.

It was Lauren who stole Stella's heart way back when Stella was only nine and Lauren was just a baby. It was Lauren who sat with her on the front porch that year she came back to Oklahoma, and without a word, gave her enough support to reopen the Brannon Inn. She sat down in a recliner and threw the lever on the side, propping up her feet and lazing back to watch the end of the first movie.

Neither of them heard the front door open but when her mother sat the bowl down on the counter, Stella opened one eye. Surely it wasn't supper time already. There was no way she could have slept through the whole afternoon without coming to even one final decision about what she would say if Rance did call again, but the clock said she was wrong. It really was five o'clock and her mother still looked like she could eat railroad ties and spit out Tinker Toys. Maggie had that smug little look on her face. The same one she had the day she came from Kansas after Stella moved back into the Inn. The "I told you so that sorry scoundrel has done just exactly what I told you and you know it and I knew anyone with all those looks could never be faithful, yadda yadda yadda," look which spoke volumes.

She nodded toward Lauren. "Hello. Don't make so much noise, you'll wake up the baby."

"She's not a baby anymore, Stella," Maggie said flatly. "But let her sleep. When we finish supper, I'll make her a sandwich to eat on the way home. It's going to be ten o'clock when we get home."

They took a seat at the kitchen table and waited. Stella pushed the foot of the recliner down and stood up, stretching all five feet ten inches of herself. She felt like she was sixteen again and late for a midnight curfew. Lucy and Maggie waited to save, sanctify and dehorn her. And when the mission was accomplished Maggie would drive away in her Bronco with a smile on her face. Younger, impulsive sister saved from a devil like her first husband; sanctified to live the life of a nun in Brannon Inn until she was old and wrinkled; and dehorned so that she would never again lust after the flesh of a well-built, good looking cowboy in tight fitting jeans and boots again.

Stella suppressed a smile and meandered to the small breakfast table in the kitchen where the judge and one man jury awaited. "Chicken salad looks wonderful. I've got tea in the pot but it's probably lukewarm. Iced tea is in the 'fridge along with an assortment of soft drinks. What can I pour you?"

"Dr. Pepper is fine." Her mother quipped shortly and Maggie nodded.

She opened the pantry and picked up two loaves of fresh bread. "White or wheat?"

Lucy nodded toward a basket and pursed her lips. "Fresh rye. Remember I said I'd bring it."

"Wonderful," Stella brought the basket to the table, along with three glasses on a tray. She went back to the refrigerator for ice, wishing she could figure out something else to prolong the conversation. She ought to tell them she and the devil-in-disguise had different views on life. She could watch relief baptize their faces and they'd all exchange whatever new gossip they'd heard.

But what if she decided she wasn't content

with the simple good-bye and wanted to see him again? Then right now was the time to speak her piece even if it hare lipped both of them and caused them to stutter for the rest of their natural lives. It all boiled down to whether or not she really wanted to bury the whole episode of Rance meets Stella. She wasn't sure, but she didn't want to make a snap decision and then have to eat her words.

"Sit down, Stella. You know that we're going to talk so stop procrastinating like your father," Lucy said.

"Why do you do that?" Stella asked. "Why do you always bring up my father when you're angry with me?"

She looked her tall, blue eyed daughter in the eye without blinking. "Because that's when you act like him. When you don't use the good sense the good Lord gave you to make decisions. Just like Dale Brannon. Always procrastinating and just letting things fall in your lap. Never looking ahead but grabbing what you want today."

Stella set her mouth in a firm line. She pulled out a chair and sat down gracefully. "Okay, your baby daughter is ready for her tongue lashing. You've got three hours. This idiot who lets people lead her around by the nose is expecting a family of twelve, arriving at eight o'clock and staying for three days. She has to finish the final touches for breakfast tomorrow morning before she goes to bed, so could you get on with this scolding?"

Maggie pointed her finger. "Don't you act like that. If we didn't love you we wouldn't care if you threw your life away with another loser again. For the love of mercy, Stella, he's a replica of Mitch and you know what that man did to you."

"No, he is not. On first impression, because he has dark hair, you might think that. But give him a chance and me some credit. I'm twenty-six years old. I'm not a teenager anymore and I know a little about people."

Her mother slapped the table. "You thought you knew about Mitch. You knew him your whole life but he sure fooled you, didn't he? You've only known this Rance a few weeks and there's that crazy look in your eyes. Mitch was just like your father. He probably played around on you from day one and it just took all those years for you to find out. This one won't be any different. Why are you drawn to men like that? Money won't buy happiness."

"Mitch wasn't rich so why are you talking about money?" Stella said. "What else have you got to say before we eat? I'm hungry and I want you to say your piece before we eat, then I don't want to hear anymore about this."

"Mitch might not have had money but this Rance fellow didn't buy the Morgan ranch with apples and oranges. So do you plan on continuing this relationship with him?" Lucy asked.

Maggie took her stand on the band box before Stella could answer. "Come on Stella. You know what a basket case you were those first few weeks after Mitch dumped you. Remember how devastated you were? Remember how bad he hurt you, and you're just now coming out of it. I was so glad when you went to Dallas last weekend for a little holiday. There're so many men in the world who'd kiss your feet. Joel's been pantin' after you for weeks, Mother says so, and you won't give him the time of day. Then this rich dude comes up here from Texas and you go all ga-ga and melt at his feet just because he reminds you of Mitch. You can't go back and redo one thing, Sister. This drugstore cowboy is cut out of the same cloth. We tried to tell you Mitch was bad news. Even Granny could see through him. At least she left you something to make a living with. So suck it up and act like the adult you are and listen to us. If we didn't love you we wouldn't be sitting here arguing with you."

"I intend to do whatever my heart tells me to do. Besides I've probably run him completely off and he'll never call again. So stop worrying," Stella said.

"You listened to your heart once and it sure made a big time fool out of you," Lucy said.

"Yes, it did." Stella nodded. "But it wasn't my heart's fault, and I'm going to listen to it again. It's all I've got to go on, you know."

"You're a foolish girl. I can tell by the gleam in that man's eyes that he's going to rip your heart out and stomp on it," Lucy said bluntly. "And when he does I promise I'm going to come and sit right down at this table and say 'Stella, you are a fool. I told you so.' I let that business with Mitch go and didn't tell you how I felt about him. Man wouldn't even marry you in our church so your friends and family could be there. Had to get married in Vegas on the way to California, and we abided by your wishes. But if you persist in getting burned again, then it's going to be 'shame on you' and I'm going to sit right here and gloat."

"Far be it from me to keep you from your gloating glory," Stella said.

Lauren sat up from the sofa where she

had awakened soon after something was said about the rye bread. "I don't know why you're on her case anyway. She made a mistake with Uncle Mitch but at least she admitted it. Lots of people make mistakes. Granny Brannon made one when she married her husband. She says he was a philandering fool after anything in a skirt, and then you married her son, Granny Lucy. And he didn't turn out a whole lot better, did he? And look at Uncle Hudson; he's divorced, too. Besides you didn't come over here and ask Aunt Stella what she thought about you dating Mr. Howard so what gives you the right to jump on her case about this Rance fellow? And Momma, why don't you go ahead and tell her why we really came down here? Daddy has a girlfriend and it looks like we might be moving back to Sulphur over Christmas break, so Momma wanted to talk to Granny Lucy about staying with her until we could get our own house. Besides, Aunt Stella isn't a teenager with raging hormones. She's got a little bit of sense, so let's have a sandwich and get on the road. I'll drive, Momma, since I've had a nap."

They all looked at Lauren like she was an apparition straight from the backside of hell. Stella's own situation took a back burner

153

and her heart literally broke for her sister. Maggie had been in love with her husband, Tommy, since they were in junior high school. Stella knew all about the fear of starting over again in the real world. She'd been there. She'd felt the pain and she wanted to hug her sister and wipe away the anguish, and put a .38 slug right between Tommy's eyes.

Maggie's voice quivered in a sob. "Middle aged crazy. He's forty one and afraid he's about to go over the hill. She's twenty three. Lord, I'm scared to death. And I don't want you to make another mistake."

"I'm so sorry. You two want to stay here?" Stella pushed her chair back and went to hug Maggie.

"No, this is your bread and butter. I can't take two rooms. I just need to stay with Momma a couple of weeks. I talked to a real estate company in town and looks like I can work there." Her voice trailed off.

"It's just that we're going to have to adjust our living style," Lauren said. "Daddy says he'll pay child support and give Mom a settlement. But it won't send me to college later on and the new bimbo wants a family so he's got to think about more kids."

Maggie shuddered. "I guess he always did want a big family, and my early hysterectomy shattered his dreams."

Lauren crossed the room and sat down in her mother's lap. "Hey, don't blame yourself. I don't think any of us here in this room have real good luck when it comes to men. I'm going to date Ricky for ten years. Maybe it's in our genes not to have a lick of sense when it comes to the male race. Now let's eat lots of fat grams and calories and make it all go away. Whatever you eat when you're baring your soul or arguing doesn't have any calories anyway."

Stella gulped and raised a well arched eyebrow at her mother. "Mr. Howard?"

"Don't you even start," Lucy shook her head violently.

"But he's bald and he wears thick glasses and he's skinny as a rail." Stella protested.

"And he thinks I'm the most beautiful thing set upon the face of this earth. He brings me bouquets of wild flowers and takes me fishing."

"And he's Daddy's exact opposite."

"Exactly." Lucy's stern mouth turned up at the corners. "I was going to tell you today anyway."

Stella still couldn't believe it. "But you had to straighten me out first."

"Did I get the job done?"

"Probably not," Stella said.

155

Lauren started making sandwiches for all four of them. "Well, at least we've got all the cards on the table. Momma's getting a divorce. Granny has a boyfriend. And Aunt Stella has a feller who looked pretty durn sexy to me. If she don't want him, I might even trade Ricky in on an older model."

"Hey, wait a minute!" Maggie's eyes widened. "I'll hear no more about that."

Stella bit off a chunk of the sandwich and used the rest as a pointer. "And I'll hear no more about school problems. We'll all rally around when it comes time for college. The world needs good doctors and you've got the brain power to be one. We'll take care of it somehow."

"I know you all will and I love you for it," Lauren said. "Maybe I'll be the first doctor to implant a devise into men's brains that makes them decent people."

"Then it will be money well spent," Stella said.

CHAPTER EIGHT

A fine sprinkling of flour dotted Stella's nose as she kneaded the bread dough. When she cooked, a job requiring no concentration for her, her mind wandered. She worried about how the pending divorce would affect Lauren, or if maybe Tommy would come to his senses. And if he did, would Maggie forgive him and take him back?

After Maggie, Lauren and her mother left at the same time last night, Stella roamed the house aimlessly. That didn't work so she put in a half hour of vigorous riding on her stationary bicycle. That accomplished nothing either. No amount of plotting or planning could help Lauren and Maggie. Why couldn't she just settle into her comfortable old routine?

Routine? That was blown to smithereens. Maggie was on her way to the divorce courts. She and Lauren were coming back to Sulphur. Her mother was dating Junior

Howard, the retired middle school math teacher? Now that was a shock. Lucy and Wes Brannon were the prince and princess of Murray County in their day. Lucy with her long, jet black hair and Wes Brannon with his Greek-god good looks. It was the wedding of the whole decade and twenty years later the divorce of that decade.

Stella frowned at the ball of dough. "But Junior Howard?"

Her mother opened the back door. "What about Junior?"

"Wow, Rance must have really spooked you. I don't see you around here for two months and then twice in less than twenty four hours," Stella said.

Lucy poured a cup of coffee. "Oh, watch your smart mouth. I wanted to talk about Maggie and Lauren and I couldn't while they were here. Started to call you on the phone last night but Junior came over to watch a movie."

Stella plopped one big white lump of dough into a greased bread pan. "Mr. Howard kept you from talking to me last night? I didn't think any man was ever going to tell you what to do again?"

"And I didn't think you were going to fall for another tall, dark man. Come on Stella, let's call a truce. I won't bad mouth that

Texan this morning if you'll leave Junior alone. I came out here to talk about Maggie. They're welcome to stay with me, but that little house two doors down from me is up for sale. To keep her from having to pay rent in an apartment, well, I've got a little put away. Maybe enough for a down payment and the first couple of payments. What do you think?"

Stella poured a cup of black coffee and joined her mother at the table. "What does Maggie think? She's the one who'll have to live in it. And it's sure not that big two story she's used to in Coffeyville."

"I haven't talked to her yet. Wanted to see what you thought."

Stella reached for the phone on the bar. "Let's call her then. Never know until we ask, will we?" The phone rang just as Stella's hand touched the receiver and she jumped like she'd been shocked.

She shook her finger at Lucy's grin. "Brannon Inn."

"Good morning, Brannon Inn." The deep Texas drawl made her blush and her mother's grin turn to an instant frown. "Did I give the guests time to eat breakfast and be on their merry way?"

She carried the phone with her as she checked the rising bread, but even that wasn't going to get her far enough away from her mother's listening ears. "Yes, you did."

"I wanted to tell you what a wonderful time I had again and ask if there's a possibility I could come over for supper the next few nights. My cook has quit and gone back to Waco. I won't be a bother. Just charge whatever you want. I only want to eat a decent meal once a day and I can't cook anything that doesn't come out of a can. Sometimes that's stretching it because I burn chicken noodle soup."

She hadn't scared him away, after all. Her heart raced like a steam engine just hearing Rance's voice. "I suppose that would be all right. Mother and I were just sitting here talking about how busy we both are."

"Aha!" He chuckled. "So did I pass muster at that little cafe or do I have to send a singing angel bearing roses and chocolates?"

"You better shine up a halo and polish a pair of gossamer wings. I had a good time this weekend, too. Actually, I figured I'd scared you off."

"You sure don't have any problem stepping up and speaking your mind, Stella, but I'm not easily scared. What's the itinerary this week? Guests have breakfast then off for the afternoon?"

She ignored Lucy's angry frowns which were supposed to make her wither up and fall into a pile of gray ashes on the floor. "I have to check. I've got the cordless phone so keep talking while I go to the living room. Okay, I've got the book. Right now I'm booked solid with part of a family reunion. Supper every night so you are in luck. They leave on Thursday and it looks like there are sixteen hunters arriving Friday afternoon so I'll be cooking for them. You've got at least ten days."

"I'll be there and thanks? Can you talk a while or do you need to visit with your mother?"

"Family crisis right now," she said.

"Want to do some winter fishing on the river after she leaves and before you have to start supper?"

"How about pond fishing? Don't know if you realize it but that farm pond at the back edge of your property is stocked too heavy with catfish so if they're not too well fed we might entice them with a good old earth worm. I haven't been fishing this winter and the sun is out today. It's supposed to be sixty degrees by this afternoon. If we catch them I'll fry them for supper and not charge you." She agreed mostly to show her mother that she could plan and run her own life —

thank you very much.

"Be there at nine o'clock?"

"I'll be ready."

"See you then," he drawled.

Her cheeks flushed with two spots of high color. "See you," Stella said.

"So I suppose that was Rance?" Lucy snipped.

"Yes, it was and I'm spending the rest of the day fishing with him." Stella dared her to argue.

"You're heading for heartache." Lucy reached for a big, round sugar cookie from the platter in the middle of the table.

"Maybe so, but it's my heart and if it aches I'll be the one who has to hurt. I promise I won't come crying on your shoulder," Stella said.

"No, you won't," Lucy informed her. "Because I'm not feeling sorry for you one bit. Now, we were calling Maggie about the house so dial her up and let's see what she thinks."

"Yes, ma'am," Stella said. The only woman in the whole world stronger than Lucy Brannon had been Audra Brannon. It would be easy to believe that Lucy was actually Audra's daughter instead of daughter-in-law. Lucy's mother, Grandma Jacks, was a little gray haired woman who never raised her voice or fought a battle. When good things came into her life she enjoyed them quietly. When bad things arrived she ignored them. How Grandma Jacks and Grandpa, a tall, dark haired gentle giant of a man, ever produced someone as sassy, brassy and even classy as Lucy had always been a complete mystery to Stella.

"Good mornin', Maggie," Stella said when she heard her sister's tired voice.

"Same to you," Maggie tried to sound cheerful but she didn't fool Stella.

"Momma is here with me and she's got an idea. But we thought we'd put it to you before we make a decision. You remember the Hatch place?"

"Of course, Mrs. Hatch died a few months ago didn't she?"

"The estate is settled. Anyway it's for sale and we thought maybe you might like to have it."

"Honey, I couldn't buy a settin' hen. There was a note from Tommy when I got home last night. While we were gone he moved his personal things out and left a financial statement about what he's willing to do. The house is mortgaged to the hilt and I sure can't keep up the payments with no job and besides Lauren is chomping at the bit to move away from here." Her voice caught somewhere between a sigh and a sob.

"Hey, sister, don't cry. Do you like that little house? It's a lot smaller than what you're used to but I think you and Lauren would have enough room and it's close to Momma and you both could come out here when town got too close for you." Stella talked fast to cover her own emotions.

"I could live in a tent on the banks of the Washita. And while I've got you on the phone, the lady at the real estate office called a few minutes ago. She said she's hiring her sister after all, so there goes my job. No job, very few skills, and no place to live. That's what I get for keeping a spotless house and making meals from scratch."

An idea popped into Stella's head, and she wondered why she hadn't thought of it before. "Maggie, Granny left me the Inn but it was because she thought I'd need it someday, which I did. But we're both her granddaughters and it's a little gold mine. I've stashed away a pretty good sized nest egg in just the few months I've been here and even you said I need to get a life. So why don't you and Lauren come work here. That way you'll have a job and I can see if I can find a life to fit me. I'm not interested in a one size fits all life and it'll have to be custom made so it might take a while." She teased to break the seriousness. "When can you get here?"

"We can stay at mother's place," Maggie sounded hopeful for the first time. "And thanks, Sis. I can certainly clean and cook. Just tell me what to do."

Stella noticed that Lucy was absolutely beaming. "That's a role reversal, isn't it? You've been telling me what to do my whole life. And you won't stay at Momma's place. You'll pick out two rooms here in the Inn and live here with me. I'll love having you and Lauren around."

"I suppose so, but don't listen to me anymore," Maggie said. "Except where that scoundrel, Lance Harpo, is concerned."

"Rance Harper is his name, and I won't listen to you there either."

"I don't even know where to begin . . ." Maggie started.

"You'll begin when you get here. When will that be?"

"We could come tomorrow. Lauren is exempt from semester exams because she hasn't missed school and has a four point. Is that too early?"

"No, it sure is not. Stay with Mother until Friday when this group of boarders empty out, but come on over tomorrow morning. We'll get an early breakfast on the table for a bunch of folks here for a family reunion. That's pancakes, sausage gravy and all the trimmings. You can make the biscuits. Now start packing up whatever you can. It'll take your mind off Tommy. We'll live through this, Maggie. We're the Brannon girls and they're made of spit and vinegar."

"Yes, ma'am." Maggie really laughed.

Lucy picked up another cookie then laid it down. It had been a tough job to fasten the button on her jeans that morning, and she'd be hung from the nearest oak tree with a rotten rope if she let herself go to fat. She'd vowed when Wes finally left with his secretary that she wouldn't let herself go to seed and weed, and she hadn't. But these past weeks of fixing extra desserts for Junior had sure taken their toll on her waistline.

"Well?" Stella raised an eyebrow. "Am I redeemed?"

"No, but what you did was very nice and I'm proud of you. You've needed help here for several months and your sister is just the ticket for that. I didn't know this place was a gold mine."

"Well, it is. I needed the twenty four hour a day, seven day a week thing to keep me bound up in my shell, but I'm ready to find that life I was talking to Maggie about, Momma. And if it takes a heart break or two along the way, then so be it. Even an ache might be better than a vacuum." She reached across the table and squeezed her mother's hand.

"Amen to that." Lucy thought of Junior and the way he made her feel like a queen on a throne when really she was just a sixty year old woman wearing faded jeans and a T-shirt and most of the time sitting on a green plastic lawn chair. "I've been in that vacuum for twenty years and it is nice to begin to find my way out of it."

After Lucy left, Stella made a hasty retreat up the steps to her room. She stripped out of her jeans and into a pair of long underwear and overalls. She tied her hair up into a pony-tail with a bandanna around it. She was putting on socks when she heard the front door open.

A voice called from the bottom of the stairs. "Hey, anybody home? Stella you up there?"

She recognized Dee's voice and opened her bedroom door. "Come on up. I'm getting ready to go fishing."

"Fishing in December? Are you crazy?"

"Probably, but I'm going anyway. Careful. Keep your hands on the rail. Good Lord, you are big as the broad side of a barn."

"Who are you going with?" Dee asked.

"Rance."

Dee flopped down on the bed and rested her hands on her huge stomach. "The married man? I saw him at church on Sunday. He's so pretty I thought all the women's panty hose were going to crawl right down their legs. But he's married, and you know that's against the rules."

"He's not married. He's divorced and the kids the hunters were teasing him about are not real children. They are his cats. Melanie and Grace. And my mother doesn't want me to go near him, so I'm going to prove to myself that I can have a life of my own."

"You surely are not going like that," Dee said.

"What's the matter with this? This is what I wear when I go fishing which is seldom anymore."

"But with Rance? Good lord, you could at least wear some good tight fittin' jeans to make his eyes pop out, or a pair of cut off jean shorts to show off your long old legs if it was summer. But striped bibbed overalls? You look like you just stepped out of one of those Farmer John commercial things. All you need is a pitchfork."

"Well, we're going fishing and these are comfortable because they fit over my long handles, and if he doesn't like it he knows the way back to his house, I'm sure," Stella said impatiently. "I promise I'll do a little better if he ever asks me out to dinner again. How about a red sequined dress slit up to my panty line and some three inch spike shoes? I could get one of those long diamond studded cigarette holders and a feather boa. Think that might work?"

Dee fell back on the bed laughing. "Oh, Stella. Rance is going to have to get up early to stay ahead of you. Shhh! I think I hear a truck coming down the lane. If he's wearing overalls, I may get another case of the giggles or start weeping. My hormones are so out of kilter, I can do either at the blink of an eye lately."

Stella's pulse raced and her head swam like she could actually faint. Why, oh why, did this particular man jack her blood pressure up thirty points? She didn't have time to take her overalls off and slip into a pair of tight jeans like Dee suggested.

"Well, he'll have to like it or leave it," she muttered.

Dee forced herself up off the bed and started down the stairs when Rance knocked on the door. "I'm on my way to Wal-Mart. Just stopped to see if you wanted to go with me. But I see you've got more important things to do. Put your boots on. I'll let him in."

"Oh, my!" he exclaimed.

"It is a bit of a shock, isn't it? But the doctor assures me there's only one in there and not a litter," Dee laughed. "Stella's on her way. She's putting on her boots."

"You're Dee, right?"

"Yes, that's me. Good luck. Don't know that you'll catch much but Stella will enjoy getting out. Now come summer time, come on up to Buckhorn and we'll show you some real fishing. Jack and I are addicts. We should have been by to welcome you to the area. I'm sorry about that but we'll come around soon."

"I'll look forward to it and take you up on that fishing," Rance smiled.

"Be seeing you. Gotta scoot if you'll clear the doorway."

"Yes, ma'am," Rance stepped to one side.

Stella was in the room by the time Rance got into the foyer. He wasn't wearing overalls but his jeans were faded out to a nice soft shade of blue and his old chambray work shirt was untucked and unironed.

"Don't you look beautiful. Got a lucky hat? If you do, you better grab it. I'm ready to sit on the side of that pond I didn't know was stocked with catfish and enjoy the day.

170

It's nippy but the sun is shining," he said.

"I've got a lucky hat and a picnic basket which should hold us over until supper time."

"Show me the basket and I'll carry it for you." He wished he could reach out and tuck that one curl back behind her ear. When he told her good-bye after church last Sunday, he fully well intended for it to be the very last one, but it hadn't worked that way. Not by a long shot. He still dreamed about her and thought about her all his waking moments. Maybe they were destined to be good friends instead of lovers. There wasn't another woman on the face of the earth who'd meet a potential boyfriend in a pair of striped, bibbed overalls and who had a lucky fishing hat.

Stella baited her own hook, which impressed him. She brought her own rod and reel, neither of which were shabby or cheap, and she had the patience of Job as she watched the red and white bobber. She sat right down on the grass without saying a word about stains on her overalls, pulled out the ugliest straw hat he'd ever laid eyes on and perched it on the top of her head.

He dropped his hook close to the edge of the pond and stretched his lanky frame out in a half-sitting, half-laying pose as he watched both bobbers rise and fall with the motion of the murky water. It had been years since he'd fished in a farm pond. The last time was when his father took him to the neighbor's ranch. Actually it was punishment. He'd been impatient with one of the horses and his father said he needed a lesson. So the next day he had the ranch cook pack them a couple of cold biscuits filled with left over scrambled eggs and bacon, a gallon jug of lukewarm water and six chocolate chip cookies. Then he and Rance went to the edge of a pond. The difference was the one back then was fairly new and only had a muddy embankment. This one had a nice grassy bank complete with a couple of old fallen logs for benches if a person got tired of laying or sitting on the grass.

Rance could hear his father's deep voice saying, "Son, we are going to fish all afternoon. When you get hungry you have a biscuit and three cookies. Don't eat them all at once. We'll just sit here until the fish bite or dark, whichever comes first, and by the end of the day, maybe you won't be so quick to fire up mad at a horse who didn't understand your command."

"Don't think about the business while you fish," Stella said softly.

"I wasn't, trust me. I was thinking about the last time I fished in a farm pond." He told her the story.

"And did you catch anything?" She asked.

"No, but I learned a lot. I learned not to let my anger control me, and I learned that my father was a salty old buzzard. I was starving to death by the time we got home and we didn't have a single fish. Know why?"

"They weren't biting," she said.

"Nope, had nothing to do with biting. The pond was brand new and hadn't been stocked, and Daddy knew it. He took a whole day out of his work to teach me a lesson, and I never forgot it." Rance watched her bobber twitch several times then settle down to the steady rhythm of the water.

"Got one down there interested," she whispered. "It'll get hungry in a little while and grab that big earth worm. Why did your dad need to teach you a lesson?"

"I let my temper get ahead of me with one of the horses we were training, and I needed to learn patience. Fishing all day and catching nothing taught me a lot."

"Oh, and you don't have a temper anymore?"

"Yes, I do, but I also have a little more patience than I did then."

173

"I see. Well, it mustn't have spoiled you for the sport. I can tell by that rod and reel and well stocked tackle box that you use it pretty often," she said.

"I do like to fish. My friends and I take boats out to the middle of a lake and fish a couple of times a month in the summer time. We have gone to Colorado to fish the colder waters and down to the gulf to do some deep sea fishing, but I haven't pond fished in years. I'd forgotten how lazy it is."

"Not lazy," she said. "Relaxing. Nothing to do but watch the bobber, pull in the fish, think about anything you want and talk about whatever. As long as it's not politics since that makes most men get loud and scares the fish off."

"Oh, come on, that's an old wives' tale. Fish can't hear us."

"Wouldn't count on it."

"So what happened with your mother today?" He asked.

"My sister is getting a divorce. She and my niece, Lauren, are moving to the Inn to help me run it and Mother is happy with me for a little while. She thinks you are the devil reincarnated and out to break my heart so we talked about Maggie, Lauren and you. And a little bit about her new boyfriend, Junior, who's a retired teacher and the spitting image of Ichabod Crane."

"Boyfriend?"

"Yep, my dad was a scoundrel, too. He left when I was young and she's been single ever since. How about your folks? You said your Dad had passed on. How about your mother? She got a boyfriend?"

"Never experienced a divorce in my family. Not until I got one. Dad and Mom married young and were still together when he died. Losing him was very hard. Thought I'd never be able to step into the business in his shoes. It's still not easy. Just because several months have passed doesn't mean I don't still think of him. Sometimes I even have the phone in my hand to call the house and ask him a question when I remember he's not there," Rance said.

She nodded. "I came out for Granny's funeral last winter and thought when I went back to California that it was all over. Put the Inn up for lease until the time ran out on the will's provisions and then I'd sell it. Then I was right back here running it and glad I hadn't been able to sell the place. But still, I turn around in the kitchen and expect to see her standing right there, shaking her finger at me and telling me how to take care of something."

Rance pointed at her line. "Granny was a

sweetheart. You've got a serious bite."

The bobber danced a couple of times then sunk like a lead weight and Stella began reeling. It was a nice three pound catfish. She brought it to shore, unhooked it from the line, put it on the stringer and staked it in the shallow edge of the pond with a stick. Rance watched her in awe, knowing that his sister, his mother or even his ex-wife would have been dancing around squeamishly demanding that he do all the things Stella just did. Then she laced another fat earth worm on the hook and tossed the line back out.

She looked down her perfectly straight nose at him. "I'm the lucky child today because I caught the first fish. So you have to take second place, but hey, something big has got your hook. It's trying to run with it. Careful now, reel him in slow. Don't let him break the line."

"I don't think I need instructions. I've caught blue marlin bigger than this."

"But not out of a pond. We may have enough for supper yet if you don't let that old grandpa break your line or maybe even the rod."

"Watch me!"

It took fifteen minutes of patience, but finally he brought the twelve pound catfish to shore and wrestled with it until he got it firmly attached to the stringer line. "Lord have mercy. I think that old grandpa is worth taking home. Matter of fact he's about worked me up an appetite. Think we could eat early?"

"Not on your life. My boarders will be in at six for supper and that's when it'll be. And honey that's not the grandpa. It's just an uncle. The old grandpa out there in the mucky bottom of this pond probably weighs thirty pounds. He was bigger than your fish back when I was just a little girl and Granny brought me over here to fish. She caught him one time and couldn't take him home for supper. Just turned him loose and watched him flop right back out to the middle," she said.

"Why?"

"Who knows? Maybe they had something in common and she wasn't ready to cash in her chips just yet either. But your fish and mine together will make enough to feed us all at supper. I'll make hushpuppies and fried potatoes and baked beans. I've already got a chocolate cake ready." She planned aloud.

She laid out a well worn orange plastic tablecloth, and opened her basket to reveal chicken salad sandwiches, chips and big oversized cookies. "And now we shall dine in style. Thank goodness we don't have to share with the mosquitoes, flies and chiggers. There is something to be said for fishing in the winter."

He grabbed a sandwich. "It looks wonderful. You must have gotten up early to get all this ready."

"No, had it in the refrigerator from last night."

"Do you ever get tired of it?" He asked.

"What?"

"The Inn. Being there all the time."

"It's my job, Rance. That's what they pay me for. Cook, clean and listen."

"Is this your job? Fishing with me since I'm paying for suppers at the Inn?" He asked testily.

"This is my afternoon off. This is not my job. This is something I wanted to do, and why did you ask me that? Are you spoiling for a fight?"

"I just wanted to know where I stand. It's evident your sister and mother think I'm a monster. Do I really look like your ex? I mean you are tall and blond like my ex, but that's where the resemblance ends. You'd never be passed off as her twin," he said.

"At first glance you'd remind a person of Mitch. But that's as far as it goes. He has dark brown eyes and his hair isn't as thick. He's not as well built as you are. He doesn't do any kind of physical work. Right now I'm enjoying this lovely day in your company, Rance. Next week we may hate each other, but today we're fishing buddies. And it seems to me that any kind of lasting thing, a lifetime thing, if you'll let me use that cliché again, maybe should start with a good, strong friendship. I fell head over heels in love with Mitch when we were in the seventh grade — looking back I don't think that was so good."

"Oh?"

"I'm not the sage of the millennium, I'm just putting into words the feelings I've had and fought with a long time. Love is nice. It's very, very cozy and warm. But like is important, Rance. Maybe as important or even more than love. I remember when I told Granny I was going to marry Mitch. She said, 'Stella Sue Brannon do you like that boy?' and I said, 'Granny, I love him!' And then she said to me, 'Love is fine and you've got to have it. But there's times when love gets thin in any relationship and like has to step in and take over. If you don't like him as well as love him, then you're goin' to be out in the cold when the love is tested.' I never knew what she was talking about until the day he came in the front door and said he wanted a divorce. I sat in the middle of the floor and finally realized I didn't like Mitch. The love had worn thin, matter of fact had played plumb out and I didn't like him. Probably never really had liked him. And those words came back to me. What she said made sense. I decided living with failure wasn't going to kill me. I got settled into the Brannon Inn rut and I don't know why I'm telling you all this, Rance. I've never gotten on a soap box twice in two weeks in my whole life," she said.

"Because I'm a good listener, and because I asked. Granny made a lot of sense. I don't think I ever liked Julie either. Boy, we did have an attraction. Couldn't be in the same room without our hormones getting out of control. But like her? Nope, I didn't. She was self-centered, egotistical and nothing was ever good enough. Me included. When the love died, there wasn't even enough to get mad about. It was like the end of a movie. We both left the courthouse, shook hands and she crawled into a big limo with her boyfriend and went back to the airport to fly to California for a photo shoot."

Stella refilled their coffee cups from a thermos. "Crazy how little things stay in your mind. I can remember thinking that

I'd wasted years on someone Granny had been right about all along."

A mischievous grin tickled the corners of his mouth. "You think you might fall in like with this old cowboy someday?"

"Don't know. I don't believe in like at first sight. You'll have to wait around in the wings and take me fishing a few more times before I know. Granny always said a good fishing buddy was worth more than a pot of gold."

"Wise, wise woman. Think we might take our lines out of the water and take a nap? I see you brought a quilt along and goodness knows nice days in December are rare even in Oklahoma. Weather man said it would get up to fifty-five degrees today and it feels like he's right for a change."

She rolled her eyes in mock horror. "Why Rance, are you asking me to sleep with you?"

"Yes, Miss Stella, I am. But sleep only. My eyes are drooping and my stomach is full. And besides I never sleep with a woman who isn't in like with me."

"Then we shall take a nap as soon as I put the remnants of this food back in the basket." Her heart soared.

CHAPTER NINE

Rance was startled awake by high pitched, piercing screams not three feet from his ear. He sat up with a jerk, looked around trying to collect his bearings and wondered exactly why he was sleeping on the ground out in someone's pasture. He turned quickly to find Stella huddled up in a ball, her knees pulled all the way to her chin, her eyes enormous with pure fright.

"Stella, what is it?"

She was sitting up but her eyes were glazed and fixed. He had a hired hand who acted just like that when he had a bad nightmare. Everyone had learned not to touch him until he was really awake or he'd come up swinging both fists.

"Stella, wake up, it's all right. Wake up," he said softly.

"I'm not asleep. Make it go away. Kill it, Rance."

"What?"

She tried to point without taking her arms away from her body. "Snake."

He looked in the direction she was staring and there was a huge black snake curled up in the sun at the end of the picnic basket. He almost laughed but decided that would really upset her. "But, it's just a black snake. They eat rats and don't hurt anyone."

"Kill it!" She demanded.

He picked up a stick, poked the snake until it awoke and slithered off toward a copse of pecan trees a few hundred feet away. Poor old snake would have to find a nice sunny spot to nap somewhere else. "Now it's gone."

"But it's still alive," she said through clenched teeth.

He tried to reassure her with a touch on her shoulder. "And it will eat field rats and other varmints."

She shrugged his hand away. "I'm not afraid of a field rat or a house mouse or other varmints. I'm scared of snakes and I wanted it dead."

"Okay, Stella. The next time you wake me up from a dead sleep screaming at the top of your lungs, I will grab the nearest club and bludgeon a harmless snake to death. I can't believe you're so afraid of a snake. You bait your own hook and even take the fish off. Bet you can even clean and fillet them, can't you?"

She carefully stretched her legs out. "Yes, I can."

"Then what's the big deal with a black snake? It isn't poisonous," he asked.

"All snakes are deadly. And there're only two kinds. Cobras and rattlesnakes," she said stoically.

"Oh, come on. There's a million kinds of snakes and more that are harmless than the bad kind."

"Nope, this is where we disagree. If it's not a rattlesnake then it's a cobra and I want them all dead. I don't care if it upsets Mother Nature's plan for the earth. I don't care if there's an overflow of mice. I'll buy rat traps or let my cat, Patches, in the house to eat them. Snakes are horrible and I hate them."

"Then we'll disagree. I just can't imagine you being afraid of anything. Does that mean we can't ever fall in like? Since you think all snakes are pure poison and I dis-agree?"

She looked back over her shoulder. "It might. But I think we're allowed to disagree on three things before we're barred forever from falling in like. And snakes is only one, so we'll have to fish a while longer and talk some more to see if there's two more."

He grabbed for a worm at the same time she did. Their hands brushed and his heart took another jolt like it always did whenever he touched her. He tossed his line out into the middle of the pond. If he caught that big grandpa he had no intentions of throwing it back in. He might put it in ice and take it home to have it mounted for the den wall at the ranch. Grandpa Catfish would have teased his last wiggle worm if he bit Rance's hook. That might be the second thing they disagreed on. "Who makes up these rules?"

"I make up the rules as I go to fit the situation at hand." She baited a hook and sent the bobble flying south of his. If she caught that big catfish her granny always said was the grandpa then she'd throw him right back in the pond. After all, they already had more fish than they needed for supper, and he'd lived in this pond longer than she or her grandmother could remember. And if Rance didn't like her decision to toss him back that would be number two.

If she fell out of like with him at least her mother and sister would be happy as pigs in a fresh mud wallow. She cut her eyes over at him without moving her head. A strand of his perfectly cut hair had flipped down on his forehead and there was a smudge of dirt on the knees of his jeans. Her gaze traveled back up his long legs to his strong chin with just a faint cleft in the middle.

He felt her staring at him but shut his eyes and pretended to snooze while he waited on the fishing rod to jerk in his hands. He didn't need to look at her to see her. Those silly overalls didn't even detract from her beauty; all that thick blond hair, big crystal clear blue eyes, and delicate features for such a tall woman. Usually tall women were a bit masculine: not actually pretty, but more handsome. Not Stella. Her skin was that strange mixture of colors he'd only seen on porcelain statues; a fine grained light flesh tone with just an extra hint of pink in the cheeks. An artist would think he'd died and gone straight to heaven to have her model. Maybe sometime in the distant future, he would ask a portrait specialist to paint her for the space above the mantle at the ranch. He'd always planned to have a picture of Count Snoopy Playboy done to fill the space. A giant picture of the horse that had put Harper Horses on the map, but no doubt about it, one of Stella in an electric blue, flowing dinner gown would be nicer.

What in the devil am I thinking about? This

girl won't even tell me she likes me and I'm already hanging her picture in the living room.

"Why do you get to make all the rules? And anyway what made you so afraid of a snake?" Rance asked.

"I make the rules because I want to. And about the snake. You ever seen a spreading adder?"

"Is that a cobra or a rattlesnake?"

"It's a cobra. Rattlesnakes have rattles and shake them. Everything else is a cobra. So have you ever seen one?"

"Of course. They're puffers. Just spread out the head as a tactic to keep away predators."

Stella shivered with the childhood memory. "Well, I was about seven and ran into the smoke house to hide from Maggie. Granny sent her outside to tell me to come to supper, and I thought I'd scare her when she came in the door of the smoke house. Only a spreading adder slithered up and blocked the door. I started screaming and Maggie couldn't rescue me. She's afraid of snakes as bad as I am. Anyway she screamed for Granny and I screamed because I was scared out of my mind. Finally Granny came running with a hoe and killed the snake. And I hate them, Rance. I really do."

"I see." He nodded and they fished another fifteen minutes in silence.

"Are you afraid of anything?" She asked.

"Failure."

"That's not what I mean. I mean anything like snakes or spiders."

"Nope, just failure, mainly, and maybe rejection which is a common thing with men folks." He watched the red and white bobber twitch then ride the gentle waving water again.

"Why is it a common thing among men?"

"Because we've got this built in thing about rejection. It's the reason we don't ask pretty girls out when we're teenagers. Fear of them saying no — I really don't know how to explain it. It's just there."

"Failure?" She frowned.

"Sure, aren't you afraid you'll fail? Isn't it a unisex fear?"

"Never thought about it. I have failed but I never thought about it beforehand. Never worried about it. Do you think that's what makes forty year old men crazy? They're afraid they'll fail? It sure can't be rejection because lots of them go after younger women at that age and most of the time they're not as good looking as they were at twenty. Tommy surely isn't. He's got a bald spot on the top of his head and wrinkles around his eyes."

"Tommy? That would be Maggie's husband?" Rance tried to keep names straight in his new world. Dee was easy to remember. She was pregnant and as big as a small Angus heifer. Roxie? Well, that woman was so flamboyant a blind man would remember her.

"Yes, it is. Something out there is flirting with your bait. Might be a turtle the way it works."

"Might be the old grandpa. Maybe he's over forty now and all the fancy little ladies in the pond have rejected him and he's heartsick."

"Probably a turtle and you didn't answer my question."

"I don't know the answer. I'm not forty and my hair isn't falling out. I do have a couple of wrinkles around my eyes if you look closely, but until we fall in like you probably won't get close enough to see them. Seriously, I don't know, Stella. I've seen it happen, too. Not only with men but women. Forty seems to be a crazy time in lots of people's lives. A time when they're finally past all the financial hardships of beginning a life together. The children don't need as much care, and there's more time for the adult. And then sometimes the man and woman find that in the working and

living, they've grown apart rather than together."

"I don't want that kind of heartache. I'd
rather live in my comfortable rut forever
than face that kind of hurt again."

He nodded. "I played basketball in high
school and I fouled a lot. Used to bother
me until Daddy told me one time that I
wouldn't foul if I sat on the bench the whole
game. Then Garth Brooks came out with
that song called 'The Dance,' and I don't
think I'm making a bit of sense."

"More than you'll ever know. It's time to
take these two fishes to the house and clean
them up for supper. I'm assuming you like
fried catfish and not baked?"

"Fried. I'm a true southern redneck. I'll
help since I'm going to be eating there
anyway."

"And I never turn down help so you'd better be ready to work."

"Sing for my supper, huh?"

"Play time is over and singing doesn't ac-
complish as much as plain old work so
forget the crooning. You can clean them out
in the shed and I'll check the roast that's
been slow cooking and get the rest of supper ready."

"Fish and roast?" Rance raised an eyebrow.

She gathered up her own equipment. "Always offer two main courses. That way if someone hates fish, they have a choice."

"Are you sure you won't shut down the Inn and work for me? I'll pay you double what you are making right now."

"No thank you. And don't be trying to steal Maggie out from under me either. She's a better cook than I am and twice as fast with cleaning, but I've hired her and if you say a word I'll poison your supper."

"You arc a vicious woman, Stella."

"Don't you forget it." She crawled over the fence without help and hiked back to the path where he'd parked the truck.

By the time she got the table set, salad greens torn and crisping, homemade yeast bread sliced and the corn meal mixture ready for the fish, he toted an enormous bowl of catfish fillets in the back door.

"Kind of slow aren't you?" She teased.

He set the fish on the bar in the kitchen and washed his hands with soap. "Hey, it's been a while and that was a big fish."

The oil was already hot so she rolled the first batch of fillets in corn meal and dropped them. They'd be ready when they floated to the top. Usually in less than five minutes. While they cooked she prepared the next round.

"What're those red flecks?" He asked.

"Cayenne pepper. Granny Brannon taught me to put it in the meal mix."

"Why? Doesn't it burn your mouth?"

"Little bit. Have to make an extra pitcher of tea every time I fix it. Years ago she and Grandpa ran a small bar and everyone in this area fishes. So once a year they'd have this big fish fry. Grandpa would cook them in a big kettle out behind the bar and everyone could eat until the fish were gone for free. They didn't charge a penny for the fish but the customers had to buy their own beer."

"Aha," Rance grinned.

"You got it. The pepper spiced up the catfish and they needed more beer to put out the fire. We don't use nearly as much as Grandpa did, but a little bit brings out the flavor of the fish." She scooped up what was ready, put it in an aluminum foil lined pan and shoved it in a warm oven.

"What else can I do?"

She pointed toward the living room. "Go watch something on television or read a magazine."

"Yes, ma'am."

They were flirting. The way his eyes flashed left no doubt that more than friendship danced in the air between them.

192

Finally the boarders came bustling into the house, kids whining about being hungry, adults worn out from a busy day. She suggested they get washed up and be in the dining room in ten minutes. They were all seated by the time she put the last of the hushpuppies in a bowl and set them on the table.

"This looks wonderful. I'm so tired of sandwiches I could die," one of the three men in the party said. "Is that real fresh catfish?"

"It was swimming in my pond this morning," Rance helped himself to three fillets and passed it on.

"Wow, you guys went fishing like in the old days?" A little boy asked.

Rance added a healthy helping of fried potatoes and hushpuppies to his plate. "Yes, we did. Stella and I caught fish this afternoon while you were off at your reunion."

"Man, I wish I woulda stayed here. The reunion thing was boring," the boy said.

"Where are ya'll from?" Rance asked.

"Pittsburgh," one of the adults answered. "I'm Robert, this is my brother, Matthew, and that's our youngest brother, James. The family all decided to come home for our grandparents' fiftieth wedding anniversary over near Davis. A bunch of them rented this lodge out south of Davis but there wasn't enough room for all of us. So some of us are at the Cahill Lodge and the rest are here. We gather up during the day at the lodge in Davis and visit. There's a pond there but we didn't bring any fishing gear and I'm not buying that expensive stuff for one week."

"You are welcome to borrow some of mine. You can buy bait in several places. I'd tell you to let the kids dig their own worms or catch grasshoppers but since it's winter, that's not a good idea," Rance said.

"Wow! Dad, can we do that?"

A lady gingerly picked at a piece of fried catfish, not sure whether to cut it with a knife or pick it up with her fingers. "You sure you don't mind? That's really nice of you. By the way, I'm Kelly, Robert's wife. This is Amanda, Matt's wife. And the red head down there is Mary, James' wife. Those two boys are mine . . . Chris and Tim. The girls belong to James . . . Lola and Macey. Not that you'll keep all the names right and we wouldn't expect you to. We'll be glad to borrow your fishing stuff if you aren't afraid they'll break it."

"If they do, it's replaceable, but I'm sure they'll be very careful." Rance looked at the boys who were both nodding emphatically.

"Us, too?" Lola asked.

"Sure. I bet I can roust up four rods by morning. They'll be sitting on the front porch."

After supper the boarders disappeared into their rooms. Stella began carrying dirty dishes to the kitchen; Rance right behind her, a load in his hands.

"That was pretty nice, letting strangers borrow your fishing equipment," she said.

"Wow, a compliment from Stella," he teased.

"I can be nice and I do appreciate it. Guess I should buy some inexpensive gear for times like this. You want to take this leftover fish home with you for lunch tomorrow?" She asked.

"Yes, ma'am," he said.

"All of it?"

"Won't let a single bite go to waste. It's my turn to fix lunch for the work crew."

"Hmmmm." An idea popped up like a flashing neon light in the back of her mind. It would throw her around Rance even more, but it would make lots more money to share with Maggie. Besides if she kept her sister busy she wouldn't have time to think about that scoundrel of a husband.

She filled plastic bags with leftover catfish. "I've got a proposition."

Rance raised an eyebrow. "What kind of proposition?"

"Not that kind!" She read his mind.

"So what kind?"

She shook a dirty fork at him. "I'm not that kind of woman."

"I'm joking. Get off your high horse and tell me about this proposition."

"Don't you take that tone with me either."

"Are we fighting? Are we out of like?"

"Right now we are. Can you hush for five seconds and let me talk?"

He loved her dancing blue eyes when she was angry. Wouldn't it be fun to live with her and have the privilege of making up every time they had a fight?

Whoa, hoss! Where did that idea come from? Stella has made it perfectly clear she has no intentions of accepting anything more than one of those lifetime things. She dang sure wouldn't move in with you. And you dang sure aren't interested in anything else so toss that idea into the trash bin and forget it.

"Well?" She asked.

"I haven't said a word in five seconds and you didn't finish. What's this big proposition anyway?"

"Maggie will be here tomorrow. I'll have lots of help so until you can hire a cook, would you like to bring the crew over here for lunch?"

Without a moment's uncertainty he began to nod before a word could escape his mouth. "Yes. Yes. Yes. You are the answer to my prayers, Stella. Bless your heart." He grabbed her in a bear hug and danced around the kitchen with her.

She was breathless when he set her down and for a moment she thought he might kiss her again, but a split second hesitation and two blinks changed the mood.

"So how much is this going to cost me?" He asked.

"How many people are we cooking for?"

"A dozen. Thirteen with me."

"Good lord. Where do you put them all? Are they all sleeping in the old Morgan house? I knew it was big but thirteen?"

"No, there's a dozen men hired to help me run the ranch. Some are ranch hands; some are horse trainers. They all have rented houses in Sulphur, Davis and Mill Creek until I can get them places on the ranch. We'll start with twelve trailer houses set around on the property. Then I'll have a house a year built to replace them. First trailer won't get here until after Christmas though. And I've got contractors coming in the spring to start the first house."

"You can't talk any of their wives into

cooking? They could bring their lunch from home."

"Trying to back out on a deal?"

"Not at all," she said.

"My grandpa does business this way. Good pay. Good food. It keeps a man happy and happy men work harder for their bosses. We've always provided a sit down meal at twelve o'clock noon. Their wives are busy with their own families and besides it would cause problems."

"Want to explain that?"

"If she got upset about something in the kitchen, I could lose a good hand in addition to my cook. I never hire relatives because of that," he explained.

"Okay then. I can't quote you an exact price because I don't know what you want on the menu. If they're going to want steaks that'll be higher than chicken and dumplings or red beans and ham."

"You fix it, honey, and send me a bill. I don't care what you cook. Just make sure there's plenty of it on the table. Whatever it costs will be well worth the price and I know you are fair."

He tilted his head to one side and their gaze met somewhere in the middle of the kitchen. Neither looked away. Something was definitely there.

CHAPTER TEN

No one should ever pack up lock, stock and barrel and leave Oklahoma because of the weather. It has proven on many occasions that it can and will change in twenty minutes. On Thanksgiving Stella's nephews had played football in the front yard in their short sleeved T-shirts. It stayed unseasonably warm all the way up to the Sunday before Christmas when one of those famous blue northers blew down from the North Pole.

Stella chose a long brown corduroy skirt to wear to church. She rustled around the closet floor until she found both of her brown suede high heeled boots. Standing there in a skirt, boots and lacy bra, she slowly slid hangers from one end of the rod to the other in search of a sweater or shirt. Finally she settled on a bulky off white fisherman's sweater. It didn't show off her figure but she wasn't trying to impress anyone that morning. She simply wanted to stay warm in the blustery north wind as she hustled from the parking lot into the church.

She flipped her hair up into a twist and secured it with a dozen pins then picked up a dark brown leather bow with a puff of illusion attached to the back. It just barely classified as a hat but it would do. Roxie, Dee's grandmother, had often reminded them that true southern women didn't enter the Lord's house without a hat and gloves, no matter what society did or did not accept. She had also told them emphatically when they first came to church with barely more than a little girl's hair bow on their heads that St. Peter would probably make them scrub the toilets in heaven for their rebellion. A hat was something with a brim, according to her.

Stella picked up a long brown suede coat and headed out the door. "I'll just be glad to get through the pearly gates with the thoughts I've been having."

Roxie, Dee and Jack were sitting in their pew when she made her way down the center aisle toward the pew right behind them. The rest of Stella's family hadn't arrived yet but they'd be along shortly. Lucy hadn't missed a church service since the day her husband left her for a younger woman.

Stella remembered that day very well. Roxie, Molly and Etta had come to visit her mother that evening when the news swept through town like a tornado. Stella, Dee and Rosie played paper dolls in the living room while the three old queens talked to Lucy. When they left she dried her tears and the next Sunday she walked into the Baptist church with a hat on her head and gloves on her hands. She claimed a pew right behind Roxie and that ended the gossip.

Stella reached up and patted Dee on the shoulder and suffered through a stinging glare at her hat from Roxie who was dressed in bright red velvet that morning. Her trademark ruffles adorned the sleeves, the peplum waist and the front of the jacket as well as the hem of the skirt of the suit. She wore a matching wide brimmed red velvet hat with a flourish of black illusion caught up in a wide bow on one side.

Even at eight and a half months pregnant Dee looked smashing in a deep green velvet maternity dress with a matching hat every bit as big as Roxie's. She looked over her shoulder and smiled at Stella, touched her hat and grinned. "Roxie made me wear it," she mouthed silently.

Stella nodded and felt a movement at the end of the pew. Expecting it to be her mother, Lauren and Maggie, she slid down a few inches further only to practically jump out of her skin when Rance sat down beside her. He wore a black, three pieced western cut suit, black eel boots and smelled like heaven.

"Mind if I sit here?" He asked.

"Free world," she muttered.

Roxie turned and narrowed her eyes. "S-h-h-h! You can talk after church."

Stella nodded. Rance raised an eyebrow. Stella shrugged her shoulders. Rance grinned.

Lauren slipped into the pew beside him. Maggie followed and Lucy sat on the end. The music director moved from the front pew to the podium and called out a hymn number. Stella and Rance reached for the last book on the back of the pew in front of them at the same time. Their fingertips brushed and they both jumped as if they'd grabbed hold of a bare electric wire. Rance turned to the right page and shared it with Stella but he was careful not to touch her hand.

Stella kept her hands clasped in her lap so tight they ached and wished she'd kept her kid leather gloves on instead of removing them and sticking them in the pocket of her coat she'd left on a hook in the foyer.

So that's the reason a southern lady wears gloves to church. Roxie didn't ever tell us why. Just that it was a disgrace for a southern woman to appear in the Lord's house on his day without gloves and a hat. Now I know. It hasn't got a blessed thing to do with looks. It has to do with keeping skin from touching skin and the thoughts it provokes.

Prayers were said. Sermon delivered. Altar call extended. Benediction given. And then they could talk but both Rance and Stella were tongue tied.

"Rance! You are finally here!" Jodie grabbed him as soon as services were over in a fierce bear hug, molding her tall, slim body into his.

"Been wondering where you were. I've been moved in for weeks now and you haven't even called." He kept an arm slung around her shoulder. "Stella, do you know Jodie?"

"Of course we know each other," Jodie grinned. "We grew up together. She and my sister Roseanna are the same age. My grandmother and hers were best friends since the sixth day of creation. Granny Etta is making chicken and dumplings. Come home with me for dinner."

"I'd love to. See you later Stella. Tomorrow at noon?" He asked.

"It'll be on the table at twelve sharp." She tried to smile but it came out more of a grimace. Suddenly she was sorry that he gave his hired help Sunday off. Only a skeleton crew did the morning and evening chores and that rotated. So she and Maggie did not fix Sunday dinner for them.

"Why don't you come, too?" Jodie asked Stella. "Ya'll, too, Roxie. Granny has enough to feed an army."

"Thanks anyway but we'll have to pass. Dee's got a cravin' for chili, cheese tator tots with mustard. She woke me up at two o'clock wanting them and I promised if she'd go back to sleep I'd take her to Jewel's Restaurant after church," Jack said.

"Well, I don't have a cravin' for any such thing and I'll love to visit with Etta this afternoon, so I'll take you up on the invitation and thank you for it," Roxie said.

"You?" Jodie looked at Stella.

"No, I hear a good book and a nap calling my name. Tell Granny Etta hello for me, Roxie," Stella escaped out the door before she turned neon green with jealousy.

A slow drizzle had begun while she was in church. She hurriedly ran toward her pickup truck. The wind seeped through her coat and sweater and she shivered, wishing she could snuggle up in Rance's arms for warmth. She should have a fling with Rance just to get him out of her blood or else give the Inn to Maggie and Lauren, get in the truck and run back to California. She could get her old job back or Tina would put her to work on her staff.

"But a southern woman holds her head high and does not run from her problems, no matter if she's walking in tall cotton or deep manure." She remembered Roxie's words.

By the time Stella had the truck's engine running, the rain had begun to freeze, a slick icing coating on every thing it touched: the hood of her pickup truck, the roads, tree limbs and pansy petals in the church flower beds. She turned west out of the parking lot toward the stop sign, skidded just slightly when she braked and reminded herself to drive slowly as she turned left into the park entrance. By the time she passed the Cahill Lodge sign with an arrow pointing back east, tears had begun to stream down her cheeks.

Jodie is so pretty and they have so much in common. Both of them are ranchers. I wouldn't be surprised if he doesn't ride bulls, too, just like she does. Why did he have to fall into my world?

She wiped away the tears and brought back a mascara stained leather glove. A black cat darted out from one side of the road and she stomped the brakes to keep from hitting it. The truck went into a slippery, long sideways slide. She eased off the brake and turned the steering wheel but it wouldn't respond to her touch. No matter which way she whipped the wheel, the truck kept sliding until it built up enough speed to do two or three complete circles in the middle of the road. When it finally came to a stop, the nose was pointed straight down into a ditch and the bed pointed toward heaven. All four tires were on frozen solid ground but Stella was shaking like a leaf in a tornado.

She touched her face and looked at the gloves. No blood, just more tears. She wiggled her arms and legs. Nothing seemed to be broken but her chest had strained against the seat belt and would be bruised by morning. She leaned her head down on the steering wheel and sobbed, not with so much physical pain or even mental, but relief that she was still alive.

Rance didn't see the cat but he saw Stella's truck go into a spin. He was a few hundred yards back and watched the scenario unfold in slow motion. By the time the truck stopped, he had found a place to pull over, and tried to run. His slick bottomed cowboy boots couldn't get traction on the icy slope and he fell twice. From ten feet out, he saw her fall forward onto the steering wheel. She was unconscious or dead and he'd lose her, all because he wasn't willing for that lifetime thing she kept talking about.

Be alive! Please be alive. I'll change my way of thinking. I promise. I love you. God, I do. I want you in my life. What am I thinking? I can't love Stella.

He jerked the door open and pulled a cell phone out of the inside pocket of his coat at the same time. He had dialed 9 and had his finger on 1 when she raised her head up. Pale as a ghost but her eyes were open. Tears streaming, but no blood. He flipped the phone shut and asked her if she was hurt.

"No, just scared to death," she shuddered. "You missed the turn to Jodie's place."

"No, I didn't. I was on my way home to change clothes first. I'm going to reach across you and unhook the seat belt. Thank goodness you had it fastened. Then I'll take you home. We can call the wrecker service to come get your truck on the way. Here lean on me. You sure nothing is broken?"

"I can walk," she declared but her high

heeled boots slipped on the frozen grass.

He held on tighter. "Stuff is slicker than snot on a glass door knob."

She began to giggle. It wasn't funny. It was gross but she'd heard Granny Brannon say the same thing and it was either giggle like a maniac or weep and he wasn't going to see her cry anymore.

The next step sent them both flailing backwards. Rance came to a stop at the bottom of the ditch on his back with Stella stretched out on top of him, her lips barely inches from his, frozen rain drops pelting down upon them without mercy as if trying to envelope them together in a solid lump of ice.

"You all right?" She asked.

"You knocked the breath out of me." He sucked wet crystals up his nose when he tried to breathe.

She rolled off him and tried to stand, only to fall again.

"Dang boots." She removed them.

He sat up and wiped his face but in seconds it was wet again with ice crystals. "You'll get frost bite on your feet."

"It's either that or lay down here and freeze to death."

"Hey, don't get sassy with me." He made it to his feet before they both slipped and he sat down hard on the earth again.

"Don't tell me what to do." She began to run up the slope, finding out she couldn't run on ice. She slipped and slid and fell to her knees twice but got up and kept going. She didn't even look back as she raced toward his truck. She jumped inside in one fluid motion and struggled to get out of a wet, cold coat.

"Don't fall off," she pleaded with her toes. "Dang black cat anyway. I should've made it a frozen dinner for the buzzards."

"Damn. Damn. Damn." The driver's side door opened and Rance bailed inside, shutting out the cold as fast as he could and trying to dance his feet warm in the carpet around the gas and brake pedals.

"Ready to go skinny dipping in Little Niagara?" She asked.

"I'm ready to go home and get in my hot tub," he answered as he started the engine.

"You've got a dinner date remember? With Jodie?"

"I'm not going anywhere. I'm going to make a pot of hot lemon tea and get in the hot tub. And you're going with me. We'll be lucky if we don't both have pneumonia," he said.

"Do you really have a hot tub?" She asked.

"I do. Mr. Morgan had one installed but

it was old and the jets didn't work any more so I replaced it. You want to stop at the Inn and get a swimming suit or are you up for skinny dipping?"

"Just drop me at the Inn, Rance. I'll just take a hot bath and drink some chicken broth."

"No deal. I saved your life. You can't die on me now. So name your poison. Skinny dipping or bikini?"

"Neither. But I do have a swim suit. You don't live in these parts without one. In the summer we spend a lot of time at Buckhorn or in the park. Are you sure?"

"Yes, but I'm not walking you to the door in my bare feet. They feel like they've got pins sticking in them right now. So hurry up." He parked the truck as close to the porch as he could and turned up the heat.

In a dozen quick, long strides she crossed the porch and was in the house. In less than five minutes she had shed her wet clothing, slipped into a pair of oversized gray sweat pants with a matching top, had on socks and fluffy house shoes. She opened a drawer and drew out a bright floral bathing suit and picked up a flannel lined denim jacket on her way out of the bedroom.

"Hat looks really good with that outfit," he said when she hiked a hip back up into the truck.

"What?"

"Your Sunday hat. Surprising enough it stayed put during all the slipping and sliding and it looks right fine with sweats," he said.

She flipped down the visor and looked in the mirror. Wet strands of limp blond hair hung around her face. Mascara ran from her eyelashes down her cheeks. Lipstick had worn off leaving a dark rim around the outside of pale lips. She looked like something that had been thrown at the dumpster after a Halloween party.

"Did you call Jodie?" She reached up and took off the hat.

"Not until I'm in dry clothes and have socks on my feet. Hungry?"

"As a bear," she admitted as he drove back down the lane and south a quarter of a mile then back into his own lane. "We should have eaten at the Inn. I've got leftovers from yesterday's lunch."

"There's only one thing I can cook that doesn't come out of a can or a frozen package but I do make a mean omelet so we'll eat at my place before we get into the tub. I can already feel those jets at work on my aching muscles. I'm glad we don't have to go any further than this. The wipers can't keep up with this slow drizzling ice."

When he parked, he grabbed up his boots and did a tip-toe dance into his house, yelling over his shoulder that she was to make herself at home and he'd be a gentleman next time.

She hurried into the open front door. It had been years since she'd been in the old Morgan place. Not since she was a little girl and Granny Brannon had brought her over to see Frank Morgan when his wife died. He'd locked up the house not long after that and moved to Canada to live close to his daughter. The place had been for sale for at least fifteen years. Frank had many offers for the house and fifty acres; even more for the house and five acres; but no one wanted twelve hundred acres and the house. Not until Rance came along.

The living room opened off a foyer with a wide oak staircase up to the second floor. Rumor had it that there were six bedrooms up there and three on the lower floor. It looked like a man's house with heavy antique furniture: a burled oak foyer table and matching secretary and a massive mahogany coffee table. The sofa was modern: chocolate brown velvet, deep and inviting. She sank down into it and stared at the empty fireplace. Maybe later they'd have a fire.

Rance appeared in the doorway. "Food first. What do you like in your omelet?"

He wore gray sweat bottoms and a Texas Longhorn T-shirt and thick white socks on his feet.

"All of it. Whatever you've got, put it in the omelet and I'll eat it. I'm starved," she answered.

She followed him into the kitchen where he took down a mixing bowl and removed a dozen eggs from the refrigerator.

"Will you chop the peppers and onions? I'll grate cheese and get the bacon cooking." He gathered ingredients and more equipment.

She nodded. He'd applied more cologne and her senses reeled. She carefully prepared peppers and onions while he fried bacon, making sure each piece was perfectly crisp. Her stomach grumbled but she was afraid she wouldn't be able to swallow.

"Did you call Jodie?" She finally asked.

"I did. She said to tell you to go to the emergency room if anything started hurting. You might have broken a rib with that seat belt."

"I don't think so. It'll bruise but it doesn't hurt when I breathe. How do you know Jodie?"

"Oh, she's the reason I'm here," he said.

"Met her about a year ago at a rodeo. She was riding bulls. Brought home the silver buckle that year and we had a few beers to celebrate. Anyway, we got to talking and I said I was looking to relocate. Sell a ranch south of Waco that belonged to my mother's grandparents. Don't know why I had the bright idea of relocating to Oklahoma. Guess it's because of the good times I had with Dad when we came up here to hunt in the fall. We always stayed with Granny Brannon for a few days and I loved those times. Anyway, Jodie said there was this big old ranch for sale not far from her place. She sent me some information and I decided it was exactly what I wanted. I came up here and took a look. Liked it so much I went back to Waco and put my place on the market. I called Frank and he said he'd hold the property until mine sold. Soon as it did I paid the man and you know the rest. Hand me those vegetables. I'm ready to flip this big old boy." He expertly tossed the omelet in the air and caught it in the skillet, added the middle ingredients and flipped it in half.

"So you and Jodie?"

"Are just really good rodeo buddies. Did you think we were involved?" His eyes twinkled.

"Wouldn't care if you were. That's your

business. But she is my good friend and I'd hate for you to give her that line about 'live with me and don't ask for more'."

"I don't think any man with a lick of sense would offer Jodie that. She'd bust their head with her fist and then drag them off to some shallow grave," he chuckled.

"That's the truth. Jodie is . . . different."

"Jodie is a wonderful friend but it would take a bigger man than me to approach her with romance. Let's sit and eat." He motioned toward two bar stools and set the skillet on a hot pad. "Plates or do we eat out of the pan?"

"Hand me a fork and forget the plates."

"I also called a wrecker service out of Sulphur and they'll be taking your truck home." He said between bites.

"Thank you," she mumbled.

If Rance hadn't been going home to change his clothes she might have been stranded in the ditch for a long time. If she hadn't been more than half mad at him she would have stuck around and talked to Dee longer and wouldn't have left before him. Was there really such a thing as fate? Somewhere in the distant reaches of the universe, had it already been decided that they would meet and fall in love?

While he ate he wondered if she'd left the

215

church in such a hurry and refused the invitation to dinner because she was jealous. And if so, did it mean she felt the same way about him as he did her?

He sipped hot coffee after he'd finished his half of the huge omelet. "So are you ready for the hot tub? I keep it filled up and ready."

"Where's a place I can change?"

"I'll show you." He led the way through the formal dining room and down the hall. "Spare bedroom right here. I'm right across the hallway."

When they'd both changed into swim suits, they opened the doors at the same time.

"Ready?" He asked when he found enough moisture in his dry mouth to speak.

"Oh, yes," she said. "Just lead the way."

She shivered when he opened the door out onto a screened back porch. Steam arose from the six sided Jacuzzi. Water bubbled like it was a living thing, beckoning them to come in and get out of the chill. Outside, the rain fell harder. Limbs on the trees had begun to grow a thick layer of shiny ice. She lost no time getting inside the tub and submersing herself to the neck.

"A-h-h-h," she moaned.

He joined her, the same sound escaping

from his lips.

"Temperature all right?" He asked.

She leaned back into a head rest and shut her eyes. This was heaven in a nutshell. "Great."

His cell phone set up a howl, the ring tone set to play Conway Twitty's "Hello Darlin'." He reached out to the white wicker tea cart setting beside the tub.

"Hello." The smile vanished. His dark eyebrows knit down into a solid line forming a ledge above his blue eyes as he listened.

"Why are you calling me now?" His tone was as cold as the ice falling outside. "That wouldn't be a good idea. As a matter of fact, it would be a crazy one. We are getting a ferocious ice storm. Stay in Dallas with your folks. It's over Julie. It's been for a long time. I haven't even heard from you for more than a year. Why now?"

He listened and stared at the wall behind Stella's shoulder.

As bad as she hated to, she crawled out of the tub, wrapped herself in one of the big fluffy snowy white towels on the tea cart and headed back toward the bedroom. He didn't need the embarrassment of another woman in the tub with him as he discussed things with his ex wife. She completely dried her wet body and redressed in her old sweats then pushed the sheer white curtains back to look out at the freezing rain.

"Sorry about that," he said so close behind her that she jumped. "I haven't heard from Julie, my ex-wife, in more than a year. I can't imagine what's going on in her life but if she's playing nice then she's wanting something and I've got nothing to give her."

Stella didn't turn around but kept her eyes on the back yard. "I understand. I suppose you should take me home."

"You got visitors coming tonight?"

"No. Not until morning. Oh, my gosh, I'd better call Maggie. If she goes home and finds my truck and no me, she'll panic," she said.

He handed her the cell phone and the lights went out at the same time. "Here's the phone. Uh-oh, there goes the electricity. We'd better light some wood in the fireplace and turn on the oven in the kitchen. It's run by gas."

Even though it was mid afternoon, the house was as dark as night. She phoned Maggie who informed her that she'd already called the Inn and retrieved the messages. The party who'd booked the next week had cancelled and Maggie wasn't about to try to drive in the sleet. She and Lauren were staying at Lucy's until it thawed out.

"You are going home aren't you? You're not staying at Rance's house are you? That could be dangerous. Mother is in the kitchen. I'm in the bedroom. She'd just die if she knew you were over there," Maggie whispered.

"Don't tell her," Stella whispered back. "There's nothing I could do if I did go home with no electricity. Here, I could at least help Rance with the chores and have warmth."

"Be careful little sister. Be sure you're not just rebounding."

"Call me tomorrow morning and give me the update on what's going on in town," Stella hung up and went into the living room to warm her hands before a blazing fire.

Rance looked up from the end of the sofa. "Everything all right?"

"Tomorrow is Christmas Eve and there's no way I'm going to get to Mother's," she whined.

"I was going to Grapevine to spend the holiday with my mother," he whined right back.

"Oh well, we'll get lots of experience won't we?"

"What are you talking about?"

"It's one of Roxie's old sayings. Experience is what you get when you didn't get what you wanted."

CHAPTER ELEVEN

A countryside covered in a sheet of ice. A big house with all the rooms shut off except the kitchen, dining room and den. A fireplace with a blazing flame. An oven which stayed turned on whether anything was inside or not. All the things that people sang songs about on Christmas Eve, but it felt more like a prison than a happy, cozy place.

Rance had pulled out the hidden bed from both the sofa and the love seat and insisted she take the larger one since it was closest to the fire. She had plenty of blankets; a soft down pillow and the embers of a glowing fire but the total quietness was eerie. Rance's soft breathing and occasional attempt at a snore was the only noise. It was still raining but so softly it couldn't be heard, freezing on everything it touched by the time it landed.

There was no way to tell time. The electric clocks weren't working. Her watch, along with a bracelet she'd worn to church, lay on the end table but there wasn't enough light to see the numbers. She'd doze for a while, then awaken with a start and try to imagine how long it was until morning. Once she thought she'd get up and read a while. That usually worked at the Inn when she had a restless night. But then she remembered there was no electricity. That meant no lights to read so she watched Rance sleep by the fire light. He slept on his side with one arm hugging the pillow. An orange cat curled up at his feet and a black and white one shared his pillow. The look in their eyes said they were protecting him from the big blond woman.

Experience! I don't want experience. I want to go home for Christmas Eve. I haven't been there for five years and I've looked forward to this. It's not fair. Nothing is fair. Most of all being in this room right now.

Sometime around morning the rain stopped and she fell into a deep sleep. She was disoriented when she awoke. After a few seconds she remembered where she was and why. She wanted to hit something, anything. How dare God send an ice storm on Christmas Eve. It wouldn't be gone by tomorrow either; she could feel it in her bones. If it weren't for bad luck she'd have no luck at all.

She slung the covers back in a snit, hopped out of the sofa bed and stumped her toe on the recliner as she stomped toward the kitchen. She fell to the floor dramatically, moaning and groaning, holding onto the throbbing toe that felt like it had been bitten off by a wicked rattlesnake. Before she could get to her feet, Rance barreled into the room.

He gathered her up in his arms and held her while she cried. "Stella, what did you do? Did you break something?"

She pushed him away, and slapped his arm hard when he tried to touch her again. "Go away. I hurt my toe and it's your fault."

"I'm sorry you stumped your toe but it's most certainly not my fault."

"Yes, it is. You moved that rocking chair. It wasn't there when I went to sleep," she argued.

"Nothing was moved. You just stumbled and fell. Now, get over your hissy fit and come on in the kitchen. Breakfast is almost ready. I was about to bring it to you on a tray when I heard a crash."

"Don't you tell me what to do. I'm mad and you can't do anything about it. I'm going to take a shower and get dressed and maybe then I'll apologize for being a big

223

baby but not until then." She stormed off in the direction of the bathroom.

"You are a lucky woman this morning because the hot water tank is run by gas and not electricity so you can pamper yourself with a hot shower. I laid some of my flannel pajamas on the vanity. I'm bigger than you but we're about the same height so you should be able to make do with them." He chuckled but kept it quiet enough she couldn't hear. She was so darned cute sitting there in a pout that he could have kissed her.

Ten minutes later she showed up at the breakfast table in his red plaid pajamas and a towel wrapped around her head. "I'm so mad I could spit. I haven't been this mad in so long I forgot when the last time was. I want to hit something. I could even slap the fire out of you for getting up so early and fixing breakfast."

"Then I'll keep my distance. I'll remember to never let you sleep late again if this is the way you wake up."

"You can take me home. I'm in a Jesus mood."

"And what is that?" He set a platter of crisp bacon and toast on the table. A pitcher of orange juice and one of milk was already there along with three kinds of jam and butter. Coffee bubbled on the back of the stove in an old blue granite coffee pot that had seen better days.

"A Jesus mood? Granny Molly said they attacked me periodically. It's when I'm in such a bad mood even Jesus couldn't live with me. You don't need that kind of company so take me home."

"If that's what you want, I'll take you home. But I'm eating first. It's my reward for burning my hand on the skillet while I cooked your breakfast. So like it or not, I'm eating."

"Good grief, Rance, I'm sorry. Is it bad?"

"No, it's just a surface burn, but it hurt like the devil when I did it. You are upset because this ice has put a damper on your plans and probably the close brush with death yesterday is just now hitting your nervous system," he said.

She folded bacon into a piece of toast. "It's like I've got this big ball of anger inside me and it won't go away. I could go outside and walk all the way home barefoot. If I breathed on the ice it would melt I'm so full of red hot rage."

"Okay, then when you finish eating, we're going to take a trip over to your mother's place. I've got chains I can put on the truck tires to get you into town. We can drive slowly. It might take an hour but at least you'll be there for the holidays."

"You'd do that for me?"

He handed Stella the cell phone. "Sure. Just eat and we'll go. Call your mother and tell her to expect us in a couple of hours."

"Momma, how are things there?" She asked when she heard her mother's voice.

"Frozen stiff. We have no electricity and this house is total electric. Lauren is reading a book under a ton of quilts. How are you?" Lucy said.

Stella pushed the mute button. "They have no electricity. All three of them are freezing."

"Then I will go and get them. Tell them to get their suitcases packed and I'll be there in a couple of hours. We'll cook Christmas here tomorrow."

"Mother?" Stella said.

Rance held out his hand. "Oh, give me the phone."

"Mrs. Brannon, this is Rance. I've got a gas cook stove, gas hot water heater and gas heater in the bathroom. I've also got an enormous den and a fireplace. If you all don't mind everyone bunking up in the den together, you are welcome here. At least we'll all be warm and have a hot meal on Christmas day. What?" He paused.

"No, ma'am, I do not expect you to walk. I have chains for the truck. It's a dual cab so there's plenty of room. I'll be there in a couple of hours and get you. Bring whatever you want. There's lots of room in the pickup bed. Okay, then. Good-bye."

He flipped the phone shut and went back to his breakfast.

"What did she say?"

"She said thank you."

She smiled. "You're a right decent fellow."

"While ago I was the devil who made you stump your toe."

"Well, your halo is a little crooked and I think I smell smoke on one of your wings but you're an all-right guy."

Stella yelled from the living room door. "Momma, where are you?"

"I'm right here," Lucy said. "In the kitchen getting things put into boxes to take with me. I've got a turkey and a ham and things to cook for tomorrow. Where is Rance? I've got a huge favor to ask of him."

"Oh, he's loading Lauren's suitcase and sleeping bag. I was horrible this morning and I think maybe he's got a set of wings under that T-shirt, Momma. Either that or he's crazy as a loon. I was so mean you would be ashamed of me."

"Jesus mood?"

"Worse. I yelled. I kicked a chair. I threw myself on the floor and pitched a fit over a simple stumped toe and then blamed him for it. I've been awful."

"I guess there's a reason God sent an ice storm right here at the holidays but we sure don't have to like it, do we?"

"No, we do not," Stella agreed.

"Hello Rance." Lucy said when Rance found his way to the kitchen. "I've got a favor to ask and you can surely say no and I'll understand. You're already going beyond your neighborly duty taking us in for the holidays and sharing your warm house."

"And what would that be?" He asked.

"Junior, the man I keep company with, is in the same boat we are. Total electric home and he was planning to eat Christmas dinner with us. It was going to be a surprise so my family could meet him. Can I invite him to your house, too?"

Stella was shocked. "Mother!"

Lucy pointed her finger at Stella. "Hush. It's taking a chunk of my pride to ask after the things I've said about Rance."

Rance chuckled. "Of course, it's fine. There's room in the truck for six. Does he live far from here?"

"Right on the way. He'll be ready, I'm

sure. He's as cold as we are. Amazing how the idea of warmth erases pride, ain't it?" She put the last package of cranberries in the box and handed it to Rance.

Rance pulled the truck up in front of Junior's house a few minutes later to find the tall, thin man sitting on the front porch. He threw his duffle bag and bed roll into the bed of the truck with all the rest of the gear and sighed when he slid into the back seat beside Lucy. "Ah, heat. It was as warm outside as inside so I just waited on the porch. Thank you, Rance, for this invitation. I'm in your debt forever."

Rance nodded. "You are very welcome and no debt. I'm glad for the company."

They made one stop on the way back to the ranch and that was at the Inn for Stella to go inside for shoes and clothing of her own. While she was in the house she checked the water in the kitchen and bathrooms, left the faucets dripping just slightly to keep the pipes from freezing and hurried back outside.

By the time they reached Rance's house and unloaded, it was time for chores.

"You ladies going to make supper?" He pulled a pair of insulated coveralls over his clothing.

"We certainly are," Lucy said. "Potato

chowder. Then we're going to attempt to make a couple of pies for dinner tomorrow before we run completely out of light. You got kerosene lamps anywhere?"

"Every bedroom has one. Lauren, you want to put your coat on and go upstairs to get them?" Rance asked.

Lauren giggled. "That sounds funny. Put on a coat to go somewhere in the house, but yes, I'll take care of it."

"Got another pair of them coveralls out there?" Junior asked.

"Sure do."

"Then drag them out. I can help with the choring and we'll get it done a lot faster. Going to use the truck with the chains?"

Rance handed him the coveralls. "No, we've got a four wheeler that gets good traction on the ice with extra wide tires and a little feed trailer we pull behind it."

Junior gave Lucy a dry peck on the forehead as he headed out the back door. "See you in a little while."

When the women heard the back door shut, Lucy pointed a paring knife at Stella. "Not a word from you."

Stella pointed back with a potato. "Then not one from you, either."

Lucy watched the two men out the kitchen window. Junior, tall and skinny as a rail;

Rance, just as tall and built like one of those body builders with big, strong arms, and broad back.

"Mother, you are looking at Junior's skinny hind end!" Stella gasped.

"So what? If you hadn't been looking at Rance, you wouldn't have seen me. Did you two really sleep in that room together last night?"

"Yes, we did. As in sleep . . . put your head on the pillow and shut your eyes. Him on one pull out bed and me on the other. And I don't want a lecture about staying here last night. It was warm here and cold at the Inn. I'm not so sure anything could ever come of our situation anyway. I want a lifetime thing and he wants a live-in mistress."

"So are you going to cave or is he?" Lucy said.

"I don't know yet. What if I do? Are you going to be awful about it? Should we talk about it?"

Lucy thought a minute. "I think it helps to talk about it. At least for us women. Men folk are different. They go do chores, fight a battle inside themselves and when they have it all worked out so they can live with it, they just go on with life. I think we need to talk about it. How we feel. How bad it hurts. What makes us laugh."

"Then let's talk. It's at least an hour until supper time," Stella said.

Lauren carried two lamps into the kitchen and lit them both even though it was still semi-light outside. "Okay, you two can talk, but there'll be no name calling and be careful with those knives. I'm going to go back up there and find more lamps. When I come back if you two are all puffed up and fighting instead of talking, I'm sending you up into those cold bedrooms to cool off."

"Okay, do you still think Rance is Mitch all over again?" Stella asked.

"I was unfair," Lucy said. "I judged him on his looks and that's not fair. You did the same thing with Junior, you know."

Stella leaned against the bar separating the kitchen from the kitchen nook. "But he's so plain and Daddy is *sooo* good looking."

Lucy browned bacon in a cast iron skillet. "So is Mitch. Guess looks ain't everything are they?"

"But Rance is better looking than Mitch." Stella argued.

"Yes, he is and twice the man. He's a nice person and I think he likes you." Lucy eyed Stella seriously.

"I could like him. But how am I to know?

232

Is it like, love or dependency?"

"Who knows, just give it lots of time."

Lauren brought in two more lamps. "Is there blood or dead bodies, yet?"

"No, they're making nice. They haven't let me talk yet though." Maggie chopped fresh parsley.

Lauren sat down in a kitchen chair. "If you're going put your two cents in the fight, I think I'd better stay right here,"

"I'm not that bad," Maggie said.

"Yes, you are. All men are reincarnates of Lucifer right now and I don't believe it. Just because Daddy is a horse's hind end don't mean they're all devils. Personally, I think Junior is a good man. Rance is very nice as well as good lookin' and he's taken all us frozen orphans into his home so we won't die of pneumonia. That puts him right up there with the angel Gabriel in my eyes, so neither one is Lucifer. Now did you have something to say, Mother?" Lauren asked.

Maggie shook her head. "After that speech, I'd be wasting my words. Stella, please follow Mother's advice and give this thing lots and lots of time. He's right next door so he's not going anywhere. Even if you decide it's like or love and not dependency, you can take your time."

"Yes, ma'am. We are a bunch of philosophical old girls, today, aren't we?" Stella said.

"Don't call me old!" Lucy said.

"Or me either," Lauren chipped in.

"You can call me that. I feel about ninety today," Maggie said.

"Momma, tell me the truth. Do you think Rance will run away if I tell him I want a lifetime thing or nothing at all?" Stella asked.

"No, I don't. I think he's your friend, and friendship is a foundation for something that really does last. Lust and love are good, but they're building blocks, not foundation material. Now, let's turn off this philosophyin' and talk about recipes and whether or not we want to make cream pies or fruit pies for dinner tomorrow. There'll be no pecan pies since the drought last year. How about pumpkin?"

"Coconut cream and cherry and pumpkin. I'm hungry." Stella declared.

An hour later Junior and Rance came in the back door, stomping their feet and shaking the shoulders of the coveralls down toward their waists.

"That didn't take long," Stella said.

"Not with help. What is that aroma? Whatever it is I'm going to eat half of it," Rance said.

"Potato chowder. That and corn bread. After last night and this morning I'm so tickled to see a stove that works I could shout," Lucy said.

"And hot water," Lauren actually moaned in appreciation.

"Sleeping quarters might be cramped," Rance said.

"Hey, they'll be warm. I could sleep on a concrete slab if it was warm. Thought my bones would break they shook so bad last night," Junior said.

"If you'd put some fat on them, they might not shake so bad," Lauren said.

Lucy gasped.

Maggie blushed.

The other three threw back their heads and roared.

CHAPTER TWELVE

Stella figured she'd be asleep in minutes after she snuggled down into the blankets spread out before the fire but she was wrong. She should have been dead tired but her eyes popped open and she couldn't force them to shut. After several attempts she finally laced her hands behind her head and watched the flames in the fireplace. Lauren and Maggie were sleeping soundly on the larger sofa bed; Lucy had the smaller one. Rance had thrown his sleeping bag a few feet back away from the heat of the fire, and Junior was snuggled down in his sleeping bag between her and Rance.

She'd been wrong about Junior. He didn't look so much like Ichabod Crane as he did a thinner version of Sam Elliott. He had a similar deep voice; his lips were a little thinner and his mustache not nearly as thick, but his gray hair was combed the same. And his eyes lit up like a Christmas tree when they looked at Lucy. Stella was almost sure that he'd let Lucy win the Monopoly game they'd played after supper by the light of the flickering oil lamps.

She tried shutting her eyes again to see if she could fall asleep but all she saw was Rance with his head thrown back, laughing at Lauren when she picked up the Go to Jail card. She blinked and there he was asking for a third bowl of potato chowder. Finally she gave up on sleep, and listened to Junior's soft snores, her mother's loud ones, Maggie's barely audible mumbling and Lauren's sighs.

She strained her ears for something from Rance; a snore, soft breathing, anything, but there was nothing. She felt movement before she saw it. A dark shadow behind the sofa moved quietly from the den to the dining room and into the kitchen. Then she heard the scratch of a match as it was struck on the side of the box. Saw the soft glimmer of light from a kerosene lamp. Heard the rustle of fabric as he pulled on a pair of coveralls kept on a hook by the back door and a thump as he shoved his foot into a work boot and a click as he gently shut the back door.

She quietly threw back her blanket and looked out the back window. He was on his way to the horse stables. Now why on earth was he out there in the middle of the night? There was only one way to find out. She moved slowly retracing his steps by the light of a full moon flowing through the window, around the sofa and the small kitchen table, across the floor and into the mud room where the second set of coveralls hung on a hook beside the back door. When she opened the back door, a cold blast of wind chilled her bare feet. Fumbling around amongst the work boots lined up next to the wall, she found a pair, but shoving her feet down into them was like putting a golf ball into a basketball hoop. She'd inherited Granny Molly's height: almost six feet. But her maternal grandmother's feet: size six. Tall women should wear at least a ten according to the clerks at the shoe stores.

She opened the door at the end of the horse stables.

"Who's there?" He called out.

"It's me," she answered.

He stuck his head out of an empty stable near the door. "Oh, I didn't know which me it was. What are you doing out here?"

"I could ask the same question of you. Is there a bag of toys hiding in the hay and you're going to don a red suit and mysteriously float down the chimney? I came to tell you not to do that. You'll burn your tush."

He smiled. "I came out because I've got a mare about to foal. It's out of season. Colts shouldn't be born in the middle of the winter, much less in the middle of an ice storm. She wasn't eating too well this evening and I couldn't sleep anyway."

"Okay, then I'll leave you alone."

"Don't go. Come on in and we'll talk."

She stepped into the empty stall. Several bales of hay were arranged two high across the narrow end. Tack hung on nails down one long side. Horse blankets were draped across bars down the length of the other side. The lamp sat on a bale of hay under the tack.

"Nice office but no view." She teased.

He made a sweeping motion with his hand toward the bales of hay. "I like it. I'm thinking of having a window installed. Have a seat. Make yourself comfortable. I'd offer you a drink but the bar needs replenishing."

She grabbed a blanket and kicked off boots that were five sizes too big for her feet, curled her feet up tightly under her and wrapped the blanket over her legs. It smelled faintly of horse flesh, saddle soap and hay.

He sat next to her, keeping a foot of distance between them, and more than a minute of silence.

"I liked the day," he finally said. "Being in the middle of family and friends like that was great. I remember when I was a little boy I had a friend who had sisters who were teasing him all the time. His mother made the worst meat loaf in Texas and her mashed potatoes had lumps the size of toad frogs but I'd beg to go over there to spend the night because of the family thing. I loved it."

"My brother and sisters are both a lot older than I am. Granny Molly said I was supposed to be the glue to hold together a broken marriage and it didn't work. So they bossed me around all the time. I hated it. Guess we always want what we can't have, don't we?"

"Are you talking in riddles or is that a literal question?"

She looked across the dimly lit stall. "Which one do you want to answer?"

"I'll answer both. I couldn't have a big family because there weren't aunts and uncles in the wings or brothers and sisters in the house. That would be the literal question. The riddle one is whether this attraction we are fighting is something that will last a season or a lifetime. I guess we could see."

"Is that a proposition?"

"I think it's a statement. This whole thing scares the hell out of me, Stella. I didn't walk into the Inn six weeks ago with intentions of finding you. I made my brags and vows about never, ever falling for a tall blond again. That was to my friends. To my heart, well, I'd sworn I'd never put it through misery again. Somehow I think this past few weeks has put an end to my boasting."

"What does that mean?" She held her breath.

He moved closer and wrapped his arm around her shoulder, pulling her close to his side. "It means I am very attracted to you."

The narrow room stayed dimly lit but somehow electricity sparkled even if it couldn't be seen.

"Your turn," he said.

"Physical attraction is like bricks made of a child's Play Dough. It's fun to play with but if you build a house on, it will collapse."

"So you're saying that we need to back off and forget this thing between us? Because there is something there. It's pretty strong. I think it even goes beyond the like phase."

241

"I'm saying . . ." she struggled with the words. "This is so difficult. I knew Mitch my whole life. We went to high school and college together. We fell in love and got married. We never analyzed a single thing. We were in love and we were going to be married forever."

"I know. Same with me and Julie. She and I grew up on adjoining horse farms. We used to say our parents made a contract before we were weaned that we'd grow up and marry. We were the darlings of the school. She went to modeling school. I went to college for business and agriculture. That should've told us something. There she was strutting down the runway in places like New York and Paris and I was hauling hay and breeding horses. But we never talked about things. We just got married and figured it would work itself out."

She snuggled down into his shoulder, suddenly sleepy. Now wasn't that the strangest thing? In the warm house, she couldn't make herself go to sleep. Out here in the cold horse stable she felt as if she could sleep until noon the next day. "Now here we are two burned people who are afraid of that big C word, huh? Analyzing every single word and nuance instead of enjoying the moment."

"Want to just see where it leads?" He tilted her chin up and kissed her. The first one barely brushed her lips and sent tingles to her toes. The second one deepened and almost blew the top off the horse stable.

"Are you content with that?" She asked breathlessly when he let her up for air.

"For now." He leaned back into the corner and stretched his legs out beside her.

She snuggled down into his shoulder and shut her eyes. Peace reigned in the little stall and they both slept.

"Look at that would you? Merry Christmas everyone. God has sent us the sun." Junior said when he awoke to the smell of coffee and the warmth of bright sunshine coming through the window.

Lucy set a cup of steaming hot coffee on the floor next to him. "Quite literally. Both as in s-u-n and in S-o-n. Merry Christmas, Junior."

"Well, well. This is right nice. Having coffee brought to me in bed. Look at this room. Everyone is up and around but me."

Lucy sat down in the rocking chair near him. "Yes, Maggie is making cornbread dressing. Lauren is working on cranberry salad and looks like Stella went to help Rance with the chores. They sure were quiet

243

when they snuck out of here. I didn't hear a thing."

"Well, ya'll are busy with dinner so I'll make breakfast," Junior unzipped his sleeping bag.

He made pancakes for breakfast and they all stopped their chores to eat but when Stella and Rance hadn't come back at nine o'clock Junior began to worry. Maybe they'd had a four wheeler wreck. Maybe one of them had fallen on the ice. Lucy told him to stop being a worry wart.

"They're grown people. Not little kids. They can take care of themselves," she said.

A cell phone ring-tone began somewhere near the refrigerator.

Lucy grabbed the phone and redialed the programmed number. "It's from Dee. I wonder if they've gone to Roxie's. Maybe . . ."

Junior chuckled. "Now who's the worry wart?"

"Hello, Dee, this is Lucy. Is Stella down there? No? I guess she's gone out to help Rance with chores. You are what? Good Lord, girl. He's doing what? Yes, I'll tell Stella. Ya'll be careful and call us soon as you can. Is Roxie going? It's there now? Okay, get going."

"What's going on?" Maggie asked.

"Dee wanted Stella to know she's in labor. Jack is afraid to try to drive her to Ardmore. So he's hired one of those medical helicopters to fly in and out," Lucy said.

"Lord, that's expensive," Maggie said.

"Not to Jack. He could buy a helicopter and never miss the money," Lucy said.

"Then why do they live in a trailer house?" Maggie asked.

"Because they want to, that's why," Lucy answered.

"Granny, Stella can't be helping Rance. Her shoes are right here." Lauren held up the only pair of shoes Stella had brought.

"Junior put on your boots and I'll get mine. We're going out looking. Now I am worried," Lucy dried her hands.

Maggie laid the knife aside. "I'm going too."

Lauren dropped the shoes in the middle of the room. "Me, too."

They donned coats and boots and paraded across the back gate and into the pasture.

"We'll start in the stables," Junior said. "That's the first building and the closest one. If they're doing chores then this is the last place they'll go." He led the way across the lawn and down a slight embankment, helping Lucy when the ground was too slick for her to maneuver down the worn path.

245

They found them wrapped up asleep in the first stall.

"Well, there was room in the inn. You didn't have to sleep out here," Lucy said loudly.

Stella jumped as if she were a fifteen year old kid who'd just been caught making out with her boyfriend on the living room sofa.

Rance yawned and stretched, not rattled one bit.

"Room at the inn? Is there a baby Jesus?" Lauren teased.

"No," Stella snapped.

Lucy's eyes twinkled. "Then I don't have to worry about something in about nine months?"

"If there's something in nine months, it will be a baby Jesus." Stella's steely blue eyes met hers in the middle of the room.

"Too bad," Junior muttered. "Chores done, son?"

"Not yet," Rance said.

"Then I expect you'd better come on up to the house and have some breakfast and then we'll get on with them. Cows and horses got to eat even if it is Christmas day." He ushered Lucy, Maggie and Lauren out and headed them toward the house.

"I wasn't finished," Lucy said.

"Yes, you were and you're not going to

246

mention it again. They're walkin' on unfamiliar ground that is even more slippery than what we are on right now. They don't need a bunch of sass or advice."

Lucy bowed up to him. "Junior, you don't tell me what to do."

"Of course I don't, darlin'. You think the same thing. You just ain't figured it out yet but you will by the time we get in the warm house."

Stella watched them go, surprised that her mother didn't attempt to send Rance with Junior while she gave Stella a good tongue lashing. She rubbed her eyes and it dawned on her that it was Junior's doing. For that, she just might accept the man.

"Good mornin'," Rance said.

"Same to you."

Several awkward moments passed. She untangled herself from him, hung the blanket up and slipped her feet into a pair of his boots. He wiggled the kinks from his back and combed his thick black hair back with his fingers.

"Why didn't you wake me up?" She asked.

"Same reason you didn't wake me up. We were both sleeping. You going to insist I make an honest woman out of you?"

"You going to insist I make an honest man out of you?"

"Aren't you glad it's modern day and not a hundred years ago? Lucy would have been carrying a shot gun and a preacher would have been right behind her." Rance grinned.

She folded her arms over her chest and glared at him.

"Do you always wake up like an old bear?"

"I'm not cranky. I'm mad."

"This early. What set you off?"

"You did. I want you to do something to make me hate you."

"What?"

"I'm mad because I really don't want to fall for you and I have and I don't want to tell you that, but I am, and I'm so angry I could just spit."

He cocked an eyebrow at her. "What do you want to do with all this anger? Shovel out the stalls? Make Christmas dinner?"

"I'm very grateful for all you are doing and have done for my family, Rance, but when the electricity comes back on, I don't want to see you for a whole week. I want to get my head back on straight. This spinning around is about to drive me crazy. I want to be rational and adult."

"Okay. What about lunch when I bring all the men over to your place to eat? You going to hide from me? How are we going to manage that?"

"I'll go to my room and Maggie and Lauren can do the serving."

"If you need a week then you can have it. It's a deal. On one condition. My grandparents on my Mother's side of the family have a New Year's Eve barn party at their ranch near Dallas every year. I'll give you your week if you'll go with me to the party."

She was stunned. She figured he'd tell her to drop dead on the spot.

"Deal," she stuck out her hand.

He shook her hand, then pulled her to his chest, tilted her head back and kissed her long and hard with enough heat to melt all the ice in Murray County, Oklahoma.

"Merry Christmas, Stella. Now let's go up to the house. I'm starving."

CHAPTER THIRTEEN

Rance told Stella to dress western instead of formal so she took a straight denim skirt trimmed along the hem with rhinestones and embroidery and matching jacket from the closet, along with a western cut lace blouse in a poinsettia red from the closet. Once dressed, she brushed her hair, letting it fall in natural curls to her shoulders. She tilted her head back and struck a pose like Marilyn on that famous poster. No, she'd never, ever pass for Miss Monroe. Not by a long stretch of anyone's imagination. Not even if they were near sighted to the point of blindness. But she'd fiddled with her dress long enough. The time had come to sink or swim and she'd worried enough for one week so she picked up her western hat and set it on top of her head, being careful not to mess up her hair. Just as she swung open the hotel door, Rance held up his hand to knock, and they were face to face.

He took her hands in his. "My, my, don't you look like a rodeo queen?"

"You don't look so shabby yourself." She started at the toes of his shiny black, eel dress boots and let her eyes slowly travel up the perfect crease in his starched denim jeans to a belt buckle with a bull rider on it. She felt a slight blush coloring her face as she blinked and went on up the pearl snaps on his pale gray shirt to his freshly shaven chin.

"Just like old James Dean himself," he said.

"Elvis," she argued. "James Dean's hair was lighter and he didn't swagger."

"I don't swagger," he drawled.

She smiled up at him and laced her arm through his. "I'll be the judge of that. Look out world, here we come."

The barn had been swept spotlessly clean and tables for four were set up with white tablecloths and centerpieces of fresh flowers and candles. A bandstand and portable hardwood dance floor were off to one side, and a whole row of tables, set up in a U shape, were covered with food. Caterers in white western shirts and black Wranglers fussed with everything from Mexican finger food to grilled steaks. There was an ice sculpture of a quarter horse on one table and one of an Angus bull on another. The whole atmosphere overwhelmed Stella so much she wanted to run back to the house, gather up her belongings and chase right back across the Red River.

The band had just finished setting up and the lead singer leaned into the microphone. "Rance Harper and his lady friend have arrived. We've got to warm up so this song's for you."

Rance gently took the hat from the top of her blond curls, drew her close to his chest and with one hand in hers and the other holding her hat at the small of her back, he nodded to the band. The first strains of "The Dance," by Garth Brooks started and she looked deeply into his blue eyes.

"Our song." He said softly.

She laid her head on his chest, listening to the steady beating of his heart as the singer told a story in song. Stella wished time would stand still and they could have the barn, the band and all those beautiful tables to themselves for the whole evening.

Rance had fallen in love with Stella. It was as simple as that. Like was fine and he'd enjoyed it. As she so aptly said that day, friendship was important in a relationship. But somewhere in all this, he'd added love to like. He could see down the lane into the future and someday he and Stella Brannon Harper were going to sit on the front porch of his ranch and watch their grandchildren, possibly even great grandchildren romp across the yard with the newest batch of puppies or kittens.

They'd not laid eyes on each other for a whole week and he'd thought of little else but her. During that time he realized he wanted one of those lifetime things she talked about. And more importantly, that C word wasn't one bit scary if he could have it with Stella.

When the dance ended, several people clapped heartily from inside the door.

A lady whistled through her teeth and yelled across the floor. "Time to share. You've had her to yourself all these weeks, and we intend to butt in." The short, slightly overweight woman crossed the barn with a parade behind her.

Rance began making introductions. "My friend, Cindy. She's married to my best friend from college, Grady. This is Stella Brannon, the woman you've all heard me talk about. This is my mother, Vivien, and this is J.T. and Imogene Grayson, my grandparents."

"Pleased to meet you all," Stella said.

Vivien shook her hand. "Rance, you failed

to mention that she was a tall blond."

"What has that got to do with anything?" Rance asked his mother.

"Not one thing. Oh, excuse us please, there's the senator we wanted to talk to this evening. Rance, there's a bit of gossip I need to share with you later. Stella, it's delightful to meet you finally. Save me an hour later or tomorrow to really visit. The people are arriving now and goodness knows we can't have anything private at an affair like this. Maybe we can have breakfast together along with Rance's mother? She's been beside herself all week just thinking about this party and you being here with Rance."

Cindy batted her eyelashes. "So why didn't you mention it?"

"What?" Rance pretended innocence.

"That she was tall, beautiful and blond?" Cindy said.

Rance slipped an arm around Stella and pulled her close. "Didn't want the joshing."

"Something like 'if I ever look at a tall blond again, shoot me and put me out of my misery'," Cindy teased.

For a moment Cindy made Stella nervous, then she realized the woman wasn't rude, just blunt.

"I've said that same line, only it concerned

a tall dark haired, dark eyed handsome man. But sometimes fate sure has a strange sense of humor doesn't it?" Stella said.

"You bet it does," Cindy said. "Now come on over here, and claim a table with me and my husband. He'll be along soon. He's even more vain than I am and always late to everything, but he'll get all that red hair to lay just perfect and then he'll join us. Rance get us something to drink."

She led the way to a table in a corner and motioned for Stella to sit. Rance headed toward the bar. Stella watched him.

"Are you as much in love with him as he is with you?" Cindy asked when he was out of hearing distance.

"I don't know about love, but I think we're definitely in like," Stella smiled.

"You look like those old pictures of Marilyn Monroe when you smile like that," Cindy said.

"You've been talking to Rance." Stella said with a snort.

He set a glass of wine in front of each of them. "What did I tell her?"

"He didn't tell me anything," Cindy said. "I didn't know if you were going to be a short, dumpy redhead or a tall brunette. All he kept saying was that we'd think you were beautiful."

"My head is swelling and I feel a blush coming on," Stella laughed.

Before Cindy could say a word and before Rance could sit down, a lady slid in next to him. She wrapped one arm around his neck and pulled his mouth down for a kiss. "Well, hello, sweetheart. Long time, no see."

"Speak of the devil." Cindy said aloud.

Rance pushed her away. "What in the world are you doing here, Julie?"

Stella looked up at the gorgeous woman, dressed in black silk slacks and a matching, flowing jacket over a lace camisole which gave sneak peeks at a skimpy black bra and the skin on her midriff. Her hair was done up in a twist, held fast with a clip of sparkling diamonds shaped like an S, with a few straight wisps escaping on her neck.

"I'm here with the senator over there. The one your grandparents are talking to so intently about boring politics. How have you been since you crossed the Red River into Oklahoma? Lonesome for me?"

"Not hardly," Rance said.

Julie turned an icy stare toward Stella. "And who's this, Cindy? Another one of Grady's friends you're fixin' good old Rance up with?"

Stella looked up right into Julie's big brown eyes. "I'm Stella Brannon. And I'm not anybody's relative. I'm here with Rance."

"Well, pleased to meet you Stella. Be careful. He's known to love 'em and leave 'em."

"The pleasure is all mine. I've heard so much about you," Stella said coldly.

"I'm sure you have, darlin'," Julie said.

She dismissed Stella with a disgusted look and turned back toward Rance. "I'll talk to you later. Oh, and by the way, I'm here with my new husband, that senator right over there talking to your mother."

"Congratulations. I hope you are both happy," Rance said.

"He'll do. The tabloids love it," she said and with the wave of a hand went back to hug up close to the gray haired senator.

"Sorry." Rance whispered to Stella.

"What for? She's just spoiling for a cat fight. Forget it. Would it be asking too much of you, since you're the host here and need to mingle with your guests, if you would dance the next three dances with me? And would you ask the band to make them all good slow two steppers?"

His eyes lit up and he led her out onto the dance floor. "You bet. I figured you'd be spittin' mad, not asking for dances."

She just smiled up at him, wrapped both arms around his neck and pressed her body close to his.

He looped his arms around her waist and pulled her tightly into his chest. "Why did you want three dances?"

"One dance would have shown her that she is obviously not in the picture any more. Two would have let her know I'm definitely with you, and three, well, just let it suffice to say, she'll know I'm damn sure not somebody's country relative being pawned off on you," Stella said.

"Is this one of those woman things I wouldn't understand?"

Stella laid her head his shoulder. "I'm afraid so. She'll stick to the old senator like glue the rest of the evening, trying to make you jealous. Trust me."

When the three songs ended, he took her hand and led her back to the table, meandering among the people along the way. There were so many she'd never be able to keep names and faces together, but that would come in time. Maybe by next year, she would have been around them all enough to call them by their first names.

Now where did that come from? It came from the bottom of my heart. I've fallen completely in love with this man, and some things are worth fighting for, and if Julie thinks she's still got a claim, she's deaf, dumb and stone blind. Because Rance is mine, and even if I have to wait for him to wake up and realize it, I will.

After the midnight count down and a kiss that rocked Stella's heart and soul, the people thinned out and the food tables looked like they'd been run over by a semi. Rance and Cindy's husband, Grady, were talking to the band members as they packed up their instruments.

Cindy sighed loudly, "I always hate to see the end. Oh, there will be a few hangers on for another hour or so, but when the band leaves, it's really over, you know."

"It's been a wonderful evening," Stella said. "I can't remember the last time I danced until my feet actually hurt, but they do."

"Rance is really in love with you," Cindy said.

"Oh?"

"Don't look so surprised. We've known for weeks, and now that we've met you we don't even mind," Cindy told her. "I really am too blunt. Everyone tells me that but I never change. If tact was money, I'd be a pauper."

Stella laughed. "I think you and I might get along just fine. I don't mind you speaking your mind, Cindy. I'd much rather someone tell me what they're thinking even if I don't like it, than wait until I'm comfortable and then spring a surprise on me."

"Amen to that, sister," Cindy nodded. "Now tell me what is happening between you two?"

Stella evaded the issue. "Oh, I think we need a lot more dances."

"I'm going to the ladies room. If I don't get rid of half a bottle of white wine and a couple of mixed drinks, I'm going to float away," Cindy laughed.

Stella stood up. "I'll go with you."

"Bad part of drinking a little too much is that it makes me sleep too sound and Grady says I sound like I'm sawing logs."

"Well, if I snore, I'm sure Rance has already heard it. Bless his heart, he took my family in to his home when the ice storm knocked out the electricity in our area. We all slept in the living room together except for one night when we fell asleep in a horse stable, but that's a long story for another time."

"He told Grady about that ice storm. If I ever lost electricity they'd have to dig a grave and put me in it. I couldn't live without a curling iron." Cindy stopped in her tracks right in front of Stella. "Uh-oh," she muttered.

In the shadows of a corner right beside the bathroom door, Julie was plastered to Rance with her arms tightly around his neck. "Come on, honey. I drove my own car since the senator had to leave early. Just one more night for old time's sake."

Cindy and Stella froze in place. Cindy had the sudden urge to wade into the middle of Rance and his ex-wife, with fists flailing and cursing loud enough to wake the dead. Just when the idiot had found someone like Stella he let that two-bit hussy turn his head.

Stella smiled and waited.

Rance growled. "Julie, take your hands off me. I'm not interested. Go on home and stop making a fool of yourself. What we had died a long time ago."

"What we had darlin' was pure physical attraction and that never dies. I'll wait in my car until the lights go out in the house and then I'll slip in your room. Your new honey won't ever even know, and what a body doesn't know, sure can't hurt them." Her words slurred slightly and she wasn't nearly as graceful as she'd been earlier in the evening.

Stella still waited.

"I want you to go home and I don't ever want to see you on the Bar H again. Get your arms from around me, or . . ."

"Or what, Rancey," Julie moved one hand slowly down his chest to his belt buckle.

That's when Stella moved.

Stella picked the woman's hand and dropped it like it was a dead mouse. "Hello, Julie, I think you're messing with property which does not belong to you anymore. I do believe it would be best if you go now before you do something you'll regret when you sober up. The senator would be disappointed if he knew what you were doing."

"Like I said, Rancey, some things never, ever die." Julie stomped away, but before she'd gotten far she turned around and narrowed her eyes at Stella. "Just remember every time he takes a business trip that I might be waiting. We were first loves and honey, they never die. And the senator doesn't control what I do."

A cold, chill started at the base of Stella's neck and inched its way slowly all the way down to her toe nails. Déjà vu. Her mind told her she should turn and run as far away as possible, but her heart said she loved him, and love was trust.

Rance put his arms around her waist. "I'm so sorry. I cannot believe she just said that. I promise I'm over her, Stella. I promise."

Cindy stepped up. "Well, I hope to hell you are! She's led you around by the nose forever, even after the divorce, and we're all sick and tired of it. Stella is the best thing that's happened to you in a long time. The woman is a witch, Stella. Just consider the source. Now I'm going to find Grady. You two better hash this out right now."

"I'll try." Stella said but her voice was hollow.

Rance didn't even know he was holding his breath until he exhaled loudly. "I think we'd better talk this one out rather than sleeping on it. But I want you to understand that I don't have a physical attraction for her anymore."

She looped her arms around his neck and kissed him. "Rance, I believe you. I trust you."

They sat on the bandstand, the only two people left in the barn, still warm from the big heaters that had been brought in for the party. He held her hand and tried to find the right words.

"I knew her forever and didn't know her at all. I've known you for a couple of months and it's like our two souls have known each other forever. Does that make sense?" He asked.

"It does."

"I've fought this but my heart won't let it be."

"Me, too. Maggie and I were cleaning one day this week and she had an old Rascal Flatts CD. Have you heard 'Bless the Broken Road,' the one they sang a couple of years ago?"

"I'm a huge Rascal Flatts fan. Yes, I've heard that song."

"It talks about setting about on a road looking for a true love and how that every lost dream led me where you are, then in the chorus he blessed the broken road that led him straight to you. Well, that's the way I feel, Rance. Looking back, I set out on a broken road and it took me on a journey that led me right back home to Brannon Inn where I found you. Every experience we've both had has brought us to this moment, and those experiences are what make us who we are today. Does that make sense?"

"Yes, it does. I guess we both traveled down broken roads. Who'd have ever thought I'd end up in Oklahoma? Guess fate brought us to the right place at the right time in our lives."

"So what do we do now?" She asked.

"You still interested in that lifetime thing?"

She swallowed hard and nodded.

"I am too."

"Is that a proposal or a proposition?"

"It's a proposal, Stella. I want the marriage license, the kids and grandkids. I want to teach my son how to ride a horse and walk my daughter down the aisle to a man who'll never be good enough for her because she's going to be the exact image of you and there won't ever be a man in the world that good. I want to wake up with you, argue with you and make up after the fights. I want all of it. I lived in fear every day that you'd send a note by Lauren or Maggie to tell me it was over and I couldn't see me without you. When I tried, it was as cold as that ice storm and as bleak as a desert. So Stella will you marry me?"

"Yes," she said simply as she wrapped her arms around his neck and kissed him, erasing all fear from the C word forever.

CHAPTER FOURTEEN

Stella's hands shook as she picked up the white daisies, tied up with a wide satin ribbon. She'd chosen a pale blue brocade western cut suit. The long straight skirt ended at the top of her new ivory satin lace up boots with a two inch dress heel, making her almost as tall as Rance. She wore the pearls Granny Molly had worn the day she married. Rance's mother gave her the handkerchief she had carried when she married Rance's father. Lucy provided something blue with the very garter she'd worn when she married Wes Brannon.

"Look at you," Roseanna and Jodie peeked in the door.

Stella held out her arms. "Rosie! Jodie! What a wonderful surprise."

"Oh, no, no hugs today, girl. We'd get make up on your dress or squish your flowers. We'll blow kisses." Jodie put her fingers to her lips and sent a kiss across the room to the bride.

"How are you Rosie? I haven't seen you in years? Did you see Dee's baby boy? Isn't he a doll? I want a whole house full just like him." Stella talked too fast to cover the nervousness.

Roseanna's eyes filled with so many tears that she had trouble catching them with a tissue. "You're making me cry," she said.

"I'm sorry. What's the matter Rosie?"

"Oh, it's not you or the wedding. I'm tickled to death that you've found someone like Rance. I met him down stairs and Jodie has known him for a long time. She says he's a good man and if she says so, then he must have a gold heart and wings."

Stella put an arm around her old friend. "Then what is it?"

"There's a situation I have to deal with but I'm not ruining your day with details. So on with the wedding. Look here, here's your father, all ready to walk you down the steps," Roseanna and Jodie headed back down the steps.

Wes smiled at his daughter. "You look beautiful. I'm glad you're getting married here and I'm glad you gave the Inn to Maggie and Lauren. It's just what she needs right now. Maybe someone like Rance will cross her path when the time is right."

"It was my inheritance when I needed it in the worst kind of way. Now it's Maggie's when she needs it. I'm glad you and mother are both here. I used to dream about a time when you two would get back together. I guess you have, kind of, only on a very different sort of plane. It seems right and fitting, somehow, that today we're all at the Inn. It's the place to heal our souls and begin new lives," she said philosophically.

"I think we've got a role reversal," he said past the lump in his throat. "You're playing the part of the parent but you're right. A place to begin new lives . . . to heal old hurts. I love you, Stella."

"I know," she smiled brightly. "Me, too, Daddy. Is Rance nervous? Lord, you'd think this was the first time around for both of us."

"I understand Rance today," he said.

"I bet you do. I bet you were every bit this nervous when you married Sandy," the corners of her mouth turned up. "And I bet Momma and Junior will find out this summer when they tie the knot. Is it time yet? Where is Momma anyway?"

"Down stairs, gossiping with Rance's mother. They've hit it off really good. Now, Sandy, she's taken to his grandmother more. A few years ago Sandy and your mother would have started the third World War if they'd had to share the same town, and now they are actually civil to each other in the same kitchen," Wes said.

She laid her flowers aside and wrung the hanky like it was filled with water. "Sometimes I wonder about how things do work out. Daddy, tell me I'm doing the right thing."

"Why? Your heart must have already told you that you were doing the right thing or you wouldn't be where you are today. It's all right to have jitters and doubts. Don't ever take Rance for granted. Love each other for today because that's all you get."

"Whew, we've talked more about heavy things this day than we ever did in our lives. You didn't tell me things like that the first time," she hugged him.

"Nope, but I should have. Mitch wasn't the man for you and I knew it but didn't think I had the right to say a word since I'd left your mother for Sandy."

Lucy spoke from the door where she'd been listening, "How right you are. Rance looks like a movie star and he's waiting. Maggie held up two fingers when I came up the stairs, so I guess that means two minutes. You should have let her stand up

269

with you, Stella. After all she is your sister."

"Rance chose his grandpa and you're my best friend, so I wanted you. Did you see Dee and Jack and the new baby boy?"

"Yes, Jaxson is too pretty to be a boy. When do I get another grandbaby?"

"Is nine months too long?" Stella teased.

"Not if it takes that long to make one as pretty as Jaxon. That Jack can sure make pretty babies. I bet Rance does a good job of it, too."

"Hey," Wes said, "you mean I don't run anyone any competition?"

Lucy hugged him briefly. "In your day, honey, he wouldn't have stood a chance. But it's time for us old dogs to step down and let the young ones have a chance. Now give your daughter your arm, and let's get this show on the road. We've got a couple of hours to drive to the reception after the wedding, and honey, me and Junior are going to show you and Sandy how to cut a rug at the dance."

"Bet me," Wes grinned.

Lucy slowly descended the stairs and took her place in front of the fireplace.

Rance waited, his eyes never leaving the staircase until he saw her at the top, dressed in blue and carrying daisies.

Stella's heart beat so fast she was afraid it

would explode before she reached the bottom of the stairs, and then it settled down to a steady thump as the distance closed between them. By the time she reached his side, every single doubt she'd had was gone. This was right and like her father said, she only had today. And today she was marrying Rance. She'd take care of tomorrow when it got here.

"Dearly beloved," the preacher said the familiar words, "we are gathered amongst a few friends and family to share in the union of Rance Thomas Harper and Stella Sue Brannon. Who gives this woman in marriage?"

Wes put her hand in Rance's. "Her family and I do. Be good to her, son."

"I will sir," Rance said

She handed her bouquet to her mother and faced Rance.

"Stella, I listened to you tell me what you wanted one day on the top of Bromide Hill. You said you wanted a lifetime thing and I'm prepared to give it to you today. My heart in exchange for yours for a lifetime. I promise to honor, respect and protect you and our love forever and ever. I give you my promise with all my love," he said as he looked deeply into her eyes.

The preacher cleared his throat. He had

not been prepared for vows at that particular time.

"Rance," Stella said, "I know I told you I wanted a lifetime thing out there on Bromide Hill, and that's truly what I want. But I want more. I want a daily thing, too. I want to open my eyes every morning to find you beside me and the last thing I want to see at night is your face before I shut my eyes. I want to realize that every day is a blessing when I can spend it with you, and so I give you my love, not just for a lifetime, but today. And tomorrow I will wake up and give it to you again."

"I accept and return the vow. Now, I have this ring which is a pledge of my love to you." He placed it on her finger and kissed the tips when he finished.

"And I have this one for you." She put the matching plain gold band on his finger. "I pledge my love to you with it, forever, amen."

They both turned to face the preacher, who smiled. "I think my job has just been finished. But I would like to say a few words," he closed his book. What he'd been about to say didn't fit, somehow, so he simply bowed his head and said a simple prayer.

"And now by the authority vested in me

by the state of Oklahoma, I pronounce you man and wife. Rance you may kiss your bride."

Stella put both arms around his neck and claimed her husband.

They were met at the barn door in Dallas by Rance's grandfather. "Half the state of Texas is in there and they're all waiting for you to cut the cake and dance the first dance so the party can begin. We got the barbecue ready and the caterers have been working since daybreak. Cake is beautiful."

Stella slipped her hand in Rance's. "Then let's go cut the cake and dance."

The barn had been transformed into a wedding chapel with yards and yards of white bridal illusion draped everywhere. A six tiered cake waited on a round table flanked by two eight foot tables on either side. One of the tables held a German chocolate groom's cake and the other a bubbling champagne fountain. Not one thing intimidated Stella like it had when she attended the New Year's Eve party. She was part of the family now and accepted by everyone.

The photographer pointed to the cake. "We'll start the pictures here. Rance put your hand on the knife first and Stella, you put yours over his. Now look right into the camera," he said and captured the moment for all eternity.

When they'd finished listening to a toast from Grandpa Grayson, one from Lucy, and still another from Cindy and Grady, the band played "Bless the Broken Road," and Rance led Stella to the middle of the floor.

She kissed him passionately to the whoops and hollers of everyone present. "What a nice surprise."

"Hey, I'll hire the band to play this all night for that kind of reaction," he said softly into her ear.

"Deal," she said.

"And now, Rance and Stella have asked that everyone join them for the last part of the song, and give them their blessing and support by finishing the dance with them," announced the band.

"I love you," Stella said.

"I thought you might, but do you like me?" Rance asked.

"Yes, sir, I truly do," she said.

They left amidst a shower of bird seed at midnight. They would spend the night in Dallas and fly out the next morning. Then they had a whole week in complete privacy with nothing to keep them company but each other.

He carried her over the threshold at the hotel, kicked the door shut with his boot heel without breaking the kiss he started when he opened the door.

"Help me get all these buttons undone," she whispered.

"All in due time," he said. "We've got a whole lifetime ahead of us."

She pushed him back on the bed. "No, honey, we don't. Some things are lifetime things. Some are right now things."

ABOUT THE AUTHOR

Award-winning author **Carolyn Brown** has written over thirty books. She and her husband, Charles, live in Texas and Oklahoma. *To Commit* is her twenty-ninth book for AVALON and the second in the *Broken Roads* series. *To Trust, Evening Star, Sweet Tilly, Morning Glory, Promises, The PMS Club, Redemption, Chances, Trouble in Paradise, Absolution, Choices, The Wager, Augusta, Garnet, Gypsy, Velvet, Willow, That Way Again, Just Grace, Maggie's Mistake, Violet's Wish, Emma's Folly, Lily's White Lace, The Ivy Tree, All the Way from Texas, The Yard Rose, A Falling Star,* and *Love Is* are also available.

The employees of Thorndike Press hope you have enjoyed this Large Print book. All our Thorndike, Wheeler, and Kennebec Large Print titles are designed for easy reading, and all our books are made to last. Other Thorndike Press Large Print books are available at your library, through selected bookstores, or directly from us.

For information about titles, please call:
  (800) 223-1244

or visit our Web site at:
  http://gale.cengage.com/thorndike

To share your comments, please write:
Publisher
Thorndike Press
295 Kennedy Memorial Drive
Waterville, ME 04901